SATISFACTION
GUARANTEED

LAUREN BLAKELY

COPYRIGHT

ALSO BY LAUREN BLAKELY

Big Rock Series

Big Rock

Mister O

Well Hung

Full Package

Joy Ride

Hard Wood

One Love Series

The Sexy One

The Only One

The Hot One

The Knocked Up Plan

Come As You Are

The Heartbreakers Series

Once Upon a Real Good Time

Once Upon a Sure Thing

Once Upon a Wild Fling

Sports Romance

Most Valuable Playboy

Most Likely to Score

Lucky In Love Series

Best Laid Plans

The Feel Good Factor

Nobody Does It Better

Always Satisfied series

Satisfaction Guaranteed

Instant Gratification (September 2019)

Overnight Service (December 2019)

Standalone

Stud Finder

The V Card

Wanderlust

Part-Time Lover

The Real Deal

Unbreak My Heart

The Break-Up Album

21 Stolen Kisses

Out of Bounds

Unzipped

Birthday Suit

The Dating Proposal

Never Have I Ever

The Caught Up in Love Series

Caught Up In Us

Pretending He's Mine

Playing With Her Heart

Stars In Their Eyes Duet

My Charming Rival

My Sexy Rival

The No Regrets Series

The Thrill of It

The Start of Us

Every Second With You

The Seductive Nights Series

First Night (Julia and Clay, prequel novella)

Night After Night (Julia and Clay, book one)

After This Night (Julia and Clay, book two)

One More Night (Julia and Clay, book three)

A Wildly Seductive Night (Julia and Clay novella, book 3.5)

The Joy Delivered Duet

Nights With Him (A standalone novel about Michelle and Jack)

Forbidden Nights (A standalone novel about Nate and Casey)

The Sinful Nights Series

Sweet Sinful Nights

Sinful Desire

Sinful Longing

Sinful Love

The Fighting Fire Series

Burn For Me (Smith and Jamie)

Melt for Him (Megan and Becker)

Consumed By You (Travis and Cara)

The Jewel Series

A two-book sexy contemporary romance series

The Sapphire Affair

The Sapphire Heist

ABOUT

Look, she started it.

She issued me a challenge I couldn't back down from. Make her purr like no man has done before.

Fine, she's my business partner's daughter. All right, I'm also working in the same damn practice with her. Yes, she happens to be my ex-fling. But that was seven years ago, and it was barely a week-long thing.

Except, Sloane is still the one I can't stop thinking of -- brilliant, sexy, captivating Sloane. Maybe a week of taking her to new heights will get her out of my head.

So what if we spend a few nights on the town too?

So what if I romance her across Manhattan? It's all in the name of scientific pursuit of more magnificent Os.

Until the rules change...

PROLOGUE

Dude-bros will tell you the pinnacle of male sexual prowess is to make a woman meow.

I will tell you, that's a dumbass metaphor.

Literal, figurative, it's complete bullshit.

Cats meow when they're hurt, hungry, or just plain chatty. A feline might be stressed, pissed, or simply want you to open the goddamn bedroom door at night.

So, the cat's meow is a myth. I should know.

But the purr? The magical, mysterious, wondrous purr? The aural indication of pussycat pleasure? That's the mission impossible a man ought to be making come to life. Cats purr for a couple reasons, but the most common one is to show they're satisfied.

Yes, *satisfied*.

That's a man's job, and that's why I don't play small stakes kitty-cat games. No cat's meows, no pajamas either. My one goal when I get a woman between the sheets is to make her so immensely pleased that she purrs.

I'm not an over-and-out type of guy. There's no one-and-done for me. I'm a believer in delivering satisfaction in every way, in and out of the bedroom.

That's exactly what I want to do with a certain someone.

Trouble is, that someone is most definitely off-limits, so it's time to put a leash on this dog.

But then I learn something wildly unexpected about her, and there's no way I can turn away from that kind of challenge.

1

She's gorgeous. An absolute stunner, with captivating green eyes, high cheekbones, and strong legs. Her silky black hair is long and luxurious. She stretches, showing off her nubile body.

I can't keep my eyes off her.

Or my hands, for that matter.

I run a palm down her back, and she arches against me.

"Doesn't she seem rather . . . lethargic?" her mistress asks, concern etched in her eyes. I peer closely at the little lady in question.

Those whiskers. That tail. "Sabrina's mood seems fine. Her heart rate is perfect. Her fur looks great. I see one very healthy pussycat. Why do you think she's lethargic, Lydia?" I ask as the silky black feline swishes her tail back and forth, rubbing against my hand on the exam table.

Lydia fiddles with a necklace that dangles between her breasts. "She's not playing with her toys much."

"Does she normally like to play with toys?"

Lydia drags a hand down her chest. "Oh, she enjoys toys so very much."

Dammit. I walked right into that one.

But I'm practiced in the art of deadpan deflection. "Well, that would indicate she doesn't need my services. She seems full of energy here. Is there something else going on at home with her that I should be concerned about?"

Lydia doesn't look at the kitty. She flicks her chestnut hair off her shoulder, her eyes pinned on me, ignoring the vet tech in the room completely. "She seems to need a little more attention. I feel like that's what she's telling me."

I maintain my completely-unaware-of-her-double-meaning routine. "But *you* give her lots of attention?"

"I do, but it's solo, Doctor Goodman. I think she wants it from others, if you know what I mean."

Yep, I don't need to be Inspector Poirot to crack the mystery of that case. I figured it out the instant Lydia prowled into the exam room with a cat who is as fit as an Olympic athlete.

I slide around her efforts with a standard vet answer: "Cats are fickle. Some want attention. Some are fine without it." Sabrina rubs her head against my hand, cranking up the volume as she marks me. But hey, she's allowed to. Also, cats like me. Dogs like me.

I am an absolute animal magnet, and the feeling's quite mutual.

"See? She likes you. She might want affection from you . . ." Lydia's eyes take a long, lingering stroll up and down my body.

Time for the full-scale oblivion shield. There's a fine line between playing dumb and looking stupid, and as a veterinarian, I can't afford to look bad in front of clients. But as a man, I definitely need to pull off the clueless-to-her-advances act with a particular kind of balance and finesse.

I ask Jonathan, the tech, to hand me a thermometer.

"Of course, Doctor Goodman," he says, hamming it up as if it's his utter delight to deliver the device.

Meeting Lydia's gaze, I brandish the thermometer with a grin. "Sabrina might not be so keen on me after this."

This is the moment when Lydia will back down, I'm sure. They nearly all do when the mercury comes out.

Instead, Lydia emits a sort of *coo*, like a songbird. "Oh, I bet she'd love that. I'm up for . . . I mean, she's up for anything."

Jonathan snickers, and I sigh. I focus solely on the cat, rather than on this cat-and-mouse game of cat-and-woman sublimation. Fortunately, Sabrina's just fine, and I tell Lydia so when I'm through with the exam. I snap off my gloves, wash my hands, and tell her to keep an eye on her feline. "If anything changes, let us know."

She smiles seductively at me. "Oh, I will. My pussycat's health is quite important to me."

Stay stoic, Malone. You can do it. You've done it before. "Yes, I can see that."

She waggles her fingers. "And if anything changes for you, Doctor Goodman, let me know too."

Blank face. I give her the 100 percent tabula rasa. "Thanks for coming in today."

"I'm glad I did." She rakes her gaze over me. "You're a regular Doctor Doolittle."

I've only been called that, oh, twelve times a day. But it's a compliment of the highest order, so I treat it as such. "Thank you."

She takes a step closer, her stare dropping down, down, down. "Or should I call you Doctor Doolarge?"

I stifle a strangled chuckle—I don't want to give her any encouragement, especially since I do like her cat, as in the actual *feline*. "Let's stick to Doctor Goodman."

After I say goodbye to Lydia, Jonathan clears his throat, adopting a high-pitched feminine voice. "Tell me, Doctor Doolarge, is it *hard* being so good-looking?"

I laugh. "It's the family curse."

"And such a cross to bear. However do you manage?"

"It's not easy. Someday, I'll teach you."

"Yes, please. I want to know all your secrets." He

shifts to all-business mode. "You have a few clients who requested phone calls."

I glance at the clock. It's almost closing time, and I have a show tonight. "No problem. I have time."

He hands me the call sheet, and I head to my office and pick up the phone. When I'm done, I swing by the front desk where Jonathan and our office manager, Sam, are debating the best spots for craft beer in the West Village.

"Hey, Doctor Doolarge," Jonathan says, leaning back in his chair, stroking a hand over his bearded jaw. "Got a hot date tonight?"

With her pink hair tied in a huge bun on top of her head, Sam shoots him a skeptical stare. "Don't ask him that. It's personal. You shouldn't pry." She turns to me, adopts a cheeky smile, then whispers, "But tell me. Are you meeting a secret lady at Gin Joint tonight?"

Laughing, I roll my eyes. "Just my sister and the mic."

"But it would make such a yummy story. Vet moonlights as lounge singer and meets the love of his life at underground speakeasy. I can see it now." She spreads her arms wide, making a marquee sign. "They'd want me to play her in the Broadway version of your life story."

Jonathan scoffs. "You can't even sing."

She shoots him a withering glare. "Please don't ruin my daydreams."

I rap my knuckles on the counter. "Speaking of dreams, I have a set tonight then a hot date with some paperwork. In fact, it's the sexiest, steamiest paper-work I've ever seen."

"Just a couple more days, right?" Sam crosses her fingers.

"Here's hoping," I add.

"Me too," Jonathan says.

I head for the door, grabbing the handle.

Jonathan calls out, "Have fun with your paper-work, Dr. Doolarge." Every syllable drips with mockery.

I will never live down this new nickname with my staff.

But if the deal goes through, I can live with it.

What's a nickname when you're about to make your dreams come true?

2

That night at Gin Joint, I sing a Dean Martin tune then slide into conversational mode, tapping a few notes on the piano as I chat with the audience between numbers. "Ever want something so badly you can taste it? Like, on the tip of your tongue?"

A handful of patrons nod, murmuring *yes*.

"And it tastes so good, so tantalizing, it's all you can think about?"

A brunette at a table near the front kicks her high-heeled foot back and forth, mouthing *yes*.

"When I get like that, that's when I need to lose myself in one particular song." I dive into Louis Armstrong's "What A Wonderful World."

As I play, I'm not only focused on the tune, but on life, and my life is good. In forty-eight hours, my business partner, Doug, will return to town. He's told me he wants to have dinner to discuss a business proposition, and that's why I've been dotting my i's and crossing my t's, prepping the paperwork so I can finalize the deal to buy out his half of the practice.

It's what we've both wanted for the last few years. What we've both been planning for. The practice will belong to me, and I can take it to the next level.

Then I'll have everything I could want: a successful business, a sweet apartment in the Village, and dates whenever I want them.

The icing on the cake is this—singing to a packed house tonight. Fine, that packed house might only be fifty people, but I don't care. I'm not trying to make a career as a lounge singer. I'm just enjoying my second-favorite hobby.

Decked out in a sharp dark-blue suit, I have the audience enrapt with old standards. Men and women sip Moscow mules from copper mugs and gin and tonics from tall glasses garnished with lime wedges. Toes tap in rhythm to the music.

As I dive into the closing number, an update on "The Curse of an Aching Heart," made famous by Frank Sinatra, my eyes land on a trio of women in jeans and black tops, likely on a girls' night out.

A pretty brunette runs her finger along the rim of her glass and bats her lashes at me. Ah, the telltale sign that tonight could be another lucky night.

"You made me what I am today. I hope you're satisfied."

I'm not saying I sing at Gin Joint a couple times a month to score.

I'm saying it doesn't hurt.

Mic and the piano, the perfect prologue to my

first-favorite hobby. But there's something I want more than sex tonight, so I'm going to be an absolute choirboy when my set draws to a close.

"That's the curse of an aching heart," I sing, finishing the tune.

"Thanks so much for coming tonight. Be sure to keep all your loved ones close. I'm A Good Man, and I'll see you again sometime."

I weave my way through the crowd, and the brunette nibbles on the corner of her lips and offers, "I can break that curse."

"Thanks for coming tonight," I say, setting a hand briefly on her shoulder, then make my way to the bar. I'm giving myself a commendation for good behavior.

"Whiskey for you," says my sister, Truly, who owns Gin Joint, as she slides a glass over. "Also, do I need to grab you by the wrists and lead you out of here right away, so you're not tempted?"

"Nah. I'm willingly leaving solo."

She hums doubtfully and lowers her voice. "I saw the gal making eyes at you. Were they full-on fuck-me eyes or were they flirt-with-me-and-give-me-some-thing-to-think-about-later eyes?"

I tap my chin, pretending to think. "I do believe they were take-me-to-your-sister's-office-and-pound-me-against-the-door eyes."

I down some of the drink as Truly smacks my shoulder. "Gross. That's seriously gross. I need to get that image out of my head, stat. Talk about paper clips."

I laugh. "Paper clips are a fantastic invention, not only known for their ability to hold pages upon pages together, but also for their ability to float."

She blinks. "Wait. Paper clips float? Is it because they're light?"

I shake my head. "Nope. It's because of surface tension. The water molecules hold tight enough to support . . ."

She waves a hand. "That's okay. That did the trick." She presses her palms against the counter. "How is everything looking for the Friday night dinner?"

I rap the wood for luck. "If all goes well, the practice should be mine, like Doug and I have talked about for years. At last, right?"

She sighs happily. "We need to celebrate. It's what Dad always wanted for you."

"I know. I'm glad I can finally do it." This has been the big dream since I left vet school—to finish what my father started. To take the step he couldn't take.

"It's going to be great." She pours herself a Diet Coke and raises the glass to toast. We clink and each take a drink. "And when it's all said and done, will you reach out to Sloane again?"

That name sends a jolt through me. "Sloane?"

Truly chuckles. "Yes. *Sloane*," she says, like she needs to remind me. She doesn't—the woman hasn't slipped too far from my mind since that one intense week together that we shared seven years ago. "Sloane, as in the woman you had it bad for once upon a time. The woman you ask me about every time you bump into her, wanting to know if I've discovered some giant loophole that would enable you to pursue her, the woman who's the reason you sing here."

I stumble back, like she just blew me over with the force of her gale-strength words. "When you put it like that, I suppose the name *does* ring a bell."

She laughs. "So, will you reach out to her?"

"Why would I?"

"Won't things change once the deal is done? Can't you finally be Sloane and Malone? Which, by the way, will never not be funny, the rhyming."

"It's a laugh a minute."

"So . . ." Her eyes widen.

I shrug. "Don't know. Hadn't thought about it."

She leans forward, a twinkle in her blue eyes, a challenging set in her jaw. "Liar."

A high-pitched voice cuts in. "Oh my God, are you guys identical twins?"

Truly rolls her eyes. She *is* my twin, and because our coloring is so similar—dark-brown hair, midnight-blue eyes—we've fielded our fair share of this ridiculous question.

I jerk my gaze to the questioner—the brunette.

"It's just that you have the same hair and everything," she says, gesturing wildly from Truly to me.

My sister answers, "Yes, we are. You might have seen us in the *Guinness World Records* as the world's first male-female identical twins."

Her jaw drops. "That is so cool. I can't believe I'm

meeting identical boy-girl twins. I thought it was always one gender only."

I point to my sister. "She had a penis in the womb. It fell off before she was born."

Truly tosses a cloth at me while the brunette stares, slack-jawed. "And you became one. One giant dick."

"And on that note, I need to go." I tug Truly in for a quick kiss on the cheek, and then I'm out.

As I head down the cobblestoned block lined with trees, I unknot my tie, humming "The Curse of an Aching Heart."

I'm lost in thought, and then, looking up, I come to a stop.

I have to rub my eyes.

I check my surroundings to make sure I haven't walked into my own dream life. Everything seems abundantly real, from the air I breathe to the ground beneath me.

And yet this is a fantasy bar none. I've definitely dreamed of those legs, that body, that gorgeous face.

Here she is, walking toward me.

The one I still wonder about.

The one who got away.

3

Sloane Elizabeth's Notes to Self on ALL THE THINGS

What sort of trickery is it for an old flame to appear even more good-looking?

Surely this is voodoo of the highest order. Some sort of spell, right? What other explanation can there be?

Malone Goodman, wearing a suit and tie, tailored probably. He belongs on a Pinterest board of hot men in suits.

Obviously, this is alchemy.

Just don't let on.

Don't let on about ALL THE THINGS.

Don't let on that you googled him.

Don't let on that you checked out his Facebook page.

And definitely don't let on that you listened to one of his songs.

You are so not thinking about that right now.

You are not thinking about that at all.

It's seven years later, and you don't still think about what might have been.

You've got this, girl.

4

Some women you never forget.

Your brain won't let go of the scent of her skin. Your muscle memory holds the shape of your body curved around hers, and your senses recall the feel of your hands in her hair, your lips on hers.

It can be months, even a year, since you've seen her, longer since you've touched her, and everything rushes back in an instant.

Every damn image collides at once in a traffic jam of sensation. Sounds, sighs, scents. Her back arching, her lips parted, her waterfall of hair cascading over my hands.

But now, she's three-dimensional, flesh and bone. I blink all those memories aside, and they take a back seat to the woman in front of me.

As I drink in the long blonde hair, the chocolate-brown eyes, a body I wanted to get to know so very badly, I'm reminded of one damn near perfect week seven years ago.

One tempting, tantalizing, torturous week. It's seared in my mind. We met at a fundraising event in Manhattan, danced, drank, laughed, and stayed out all night. In the seven days that followed, we embodied infatuation. Late nights, lingering calls, chats you never wanted to end. So many sparks you could light up the night sky.

I can recall every moment, I swear.

Including the ending.

The bitter realization of who she was.

One more step, then another, and she stops in front of me, looking impossibly sexy, and she was the sexiest woman I'd ever known when she was a mere twenty-two.

But now? Dear God. She's not even dressed up. Sloane Elizabeth is decked out in exercise pants, running shoes, and a sporty tank, and I still want to lick and kiss every inch of her. A canvas bag is slung over her shoulder.

I gesture to it. "You're still shopping at midnight?"

"It's the best time to go." She raises her hands in fists. "I don't have to fight anyone over the last head of radicchio."

"I bet you don't have to arm wrestle anyone for radicchio during the daylight hours either."

"True," she says with a laugh, then eyes me up and down. Those brown irises. Those red lips. God, I remember exactly how they taste. She punches my arm, knocking my thoughts from the dirty zone to the buddy level. "How the hell are you, Malone?"

"I can't complain. And you? I take it from the grocery bag on your shoulder that you're living here. Did you move from Connecticut?" She's lived an hour or so from the city for the last several years, first New Jersey, then Connecticut, so I've run into her every now and then. But it's been a little over a year since the last time.

"I did. I'm working here now." She shifts her weight to her left leg, her soulful eyes never leaving my face. "What has it been? A year or so?"

A year and two months. We bumped into each other at a Moroccan restaurant in Chelsea that Truly dragged me to because the drinks were legendary. Sloane was dining with some hipster wannabe with a dangling earring who was clearly an asshole. Who else wears dangling earrings? She introduced me to him that night. His name was Plant. Or Brick. Or something painfully trendy that made me dislike him even more. She was still living in Connecticut at the time, so she obviously took the train into the city to see him. That tipped the scales to loathing for Dangling Earring Boy, who was also too young for her.

Her father would have hated him.

Her father hated everyone she dated.

He once remarked after she'd stopped by the office that he despised the guy she was seeing. No one was good enough for her, he'd said. I'd arched a brow asking, "No one?"

He shot bullets with his eyes. "No one, Casanova."

That was years ago, but it was all he needed to say, especially since he'd already told me not to get any ideas. When the man who signs your paycheck makes it clear his daughter is off-limits, something you already knew by virtue of the fact that BUSINESS PARTNERS' DAUGHTERS ARE OFF-LIMITS, you listen. You take it to heart.

I remember his warnings perfectly, just like I remember all the times I've seen her. "A year or so ago. Yes. It was something like that," I say, answering her question. The truth is I could give her chapter and verse of all the times I've seen her since we met—the time in Grand Central; the anniversary party her dad threw; an awards ceremony where I was tempted, so damn tempted; and the time she stopped by the office when her dad made the comment. Instead, I gesture to her getup. "So what are you doing in the city these days?"

"I just started an animal rescue here. About a month ago, and I'm getting it off the ground."

I'm surprised her dad hadn't mentioned it, even though the rescue is in its early days. But a smile takes over my face. "That's great. You always wanted to."

"I did. And I'm glad to do it. It's hard work, but so rewarding. I'm actually living in Brooklyn, in the tiniest place imaginable. But I was shopping here because I'm staying with a friend in the city tonight. Do you still have Evil Genius?" she asks.

The sneaky orange senior cat I adopted several years ago skulks through my memory. He was the wiliest cat around, slinking into cupboards and inside cabinets, even in his old age. I had him for the last five years of his life. "Nope. He crossed the rainbow bridge a few years ago. Good cat. He had a nice, long, and happy life."

She touches my elbow. "He did. You were good to him, though I'm sorry to hear he's gone. Is there a new cat in your life?"

I shake my head. "Not yet."

"Such restraint."

"I know," I say with a chuckle.

"But then, you always did have good restraint."

"And so did you."

She grins, a little flirty. "One of my great regrets." Okay, maybe a lot flirty.

She tips her chin at my jacket, shifting gears immediately. "Nice duds. What are you doing in that suit?"

I run a hand down the silk of my royal-blue tie. "I sing now at Gin Joint. A few other places too, now and then."

Her lips quirk up. "Is that so?"

"Yeah, I decided to take it up. Someone once told me I should." Ha. Take that, Plant Brick. I bet he doesn't sing, or wear a suit, or run his own motherfucking business. I bet he can't remove ovaries from a cat either.

"I'm glad you listened to that someone. That someone always liked the way you sang," she says, using her sexy bedroom voice, and I don't even care if Plant Brick is the regular recipient of that smoky, sexy tone of hers. I'll enjoy it right now, thank you very much.

"That someone has excellent taste."

Sloane smiles, a bright, gorgeous grin that threatens to rattle loose words. Words like *What are you doing right now?* and *Go home with me.*

"I do have good taste." Her gaze lingers on my face, her eyes locked with mine. The air between us crackles, and for a moment, we're the only ones in New York City. "I *still* do," she adds.

Dear God. Plant Brick doesn't deserve this woman.

I do.

I fucking do.

I step closer and lift a hand, every instinct telling me to haul her into my arms and kiss the breath out of her.

I don't, because Truly's wrong. Sure, the score might technically change when the deal's done. Her dad won't be my business partner once he officially asks me to take over the business, as I suspect he'll do on Friday night.

But Doug has also been my mentor. We have a long history. He taught me how to run a practice from the ground up. He's a guiding force in the work I do, and my work is everything. Even if we're no longer business partners, I have a feeling his daughter would still be off-limits.

I backpedal, digging my feet into the ground, stuffing my hands into the pockets of my suit pants. "We should . . . have lunch," I offer, because lunch is harmless.

"Lunch?" She asks the question as if I'd suggested we take up crocheting. "Really?"

I decide to make light of it. "What's wrong with lunch? What did lunch ever do to you?"

She hums, as if she's considering it. Then she lowers her voice, like she's sharing a tawdry secret. "Sometimes lunch disappoints. What if there's no burger or fries? What if you can't get the toasted panini of your dreams? Lunch can get you down."

"Let's do breakfast, then. It's a satisfaction guaranteed kind of meal," I say, playing along, since I don't want to say goodnight to her.

"Do you still love pancakes?"

"Do I look like the kind of guy who hates pancakes?"

She studies me once more, her gaze traveling over my clothes. Then she drops the routine. "You don't look like you hate pancakes. But, Malone, you know exactly why we shouldn't do that."

I do know.

I know it too well.

But seeing her tugs on something inside me.

Tugs on my desire to finish all our unfinished business. And yeah, it tugs on other parts too. She's more tempting now than she was the night I met her. I don't know how that's possible, but it is.

I drop all the teasing and the innuendo. "You look amazing, Sloane."

She gestures to her casual gear. "I'm super fancy too."

"You never needed fancy clothes to look great."

"Thank you," she whispers, then she runs a hand down my tie for a second before dropping it. "And you are rocking the hell out of that suit. How was your set?"

"I sang some songs, earned some claps. You should come see me sometime." There I go again, leaving a morsel I shouldn't be leaving.

"Should I?"

"You should."

"Will you get me a backstage pass?"

"You hardly need one, but I'd be happy to go to the nearest FedEx and mock one up for you."

"Will it say *A Good Man Groupie?*"

A devilish smirk takes over my face. "You know my stage name." This delights me immeasurably.

A fierce blush speeds over her cheeks. "Fine. I looked you up," she says softly under her breath, as if the admission costs her something.

I lean forward, and even though it's been a while since I've checked her out online, I throw in my confession too. "Moment of truth: I look you up sometimes too."

"Is that so?" Her voice is breathy with a hint of longing.

"It is very much so. I'm a visual guy. I enjoy the photos."

"Any in particular?"

"All in particular."

She bites her lip, lowers her face. "I wish you hadn't said that."

But she doesn't seem like she wishes that. She doesn't seem like she misses her dangling earring friend too much either. Nor do I.

Maybe it's the moonlight.

Maybe it's the sheer surprise of running into her tonight.

Or maybe it's just that she's as irresistible now as she was seven years ago.

I reach for her face, lift up her chin, and meet her gaze. "Sloane Elizabeth, you're still the most alluring woman I've ever met."

They're only words. I don't have to act on them. But saying them feels so fucking good. Hell, saying them is a massive turn-on.

Because of how she reacts.

How she trembles under my touch.

Her eyes darken as she stares at me. "Is that so? Am I like champagne?" It's a challenge. A throwdown, it seems, as she sends me back in time to the evening we met.

"You're a champagne kind of woman. A good glass of champagne delights all your senses. It tickles your nose, and it goes to your head, and it makes you just the right kind of buzzed," I say, telling her what I told her that night, feeling nearly as buzzed on her now as I did then.

She swallows, looks away, then back to me, taking a deep breath as if she's centering herself. "Malone, I can't stand here on the street and flirt with you. You can't just bump into me and make yourself irresistible again."

My lips curve up. My skin sizzles. "Am I? Irresistible?"

"You know you were."

"*Were. Are.* Which one?"

She sets a hand on my chest. "You were. You are. And nothing has technically changed."

"I'm well aware of that. And yet I still like pancakes."

"Same here." It's barely a whisper.

She rises on tiptoe and drops a searing, sugar-sweet kiss on my lips. She tastes like honey and fire, and the mere brush of her lips on mine is electric. My bones crackle and hum. For a few intense seconds, I deepen the kiss. As I capture her mouth, she melts against me like she used to.

But she breaks the kiss and curls a hand around my shoulder. "If I stand here any longer, the next thing we know, we'll be having pancakes." She lets go of me, shoves her bag up her shoulder, and turns the other way.

"Breakfast. I'm going to call you," I say.

She waves without looking back.

I walk away too, because she's right.

She's not a woman I can call. She's a woman I need to resist, even when she's no longer my business partner's daughter.

And that kiss was more of a goodbye than a hello.

5

Sloane Elizabeth's Voice Memo to Self on ONE PARTICULAR THING

Okay, so we've established a few things now.

You clearly don't have the antidote yet to the too-sexy-hot-sweet-seductive-clever-witty old flame. Find that. Like, now. Get on that, right away.

But take a deep breath.

All in all, you did fine.

Well, maybe *fine* isn't the right adjective. *Fine* is a B-minus. Your grade was more like a C on the test of self-restraint. Actually, a D-plus. A D-plus says you sucked . . . but you sucked with style.

The only reason you didn't fail is that you didn't completely reveal every single detail of your rich inner life when it comes to that man.

Why don't you just tell him he inspired a pair of

socks you designed too? The ones with the words *You're Irresistible and You Know It* on them.

Just keep that tidbit close to the chest, okay?

Maybe you should make a new pair for yourself —*Resist. Resist Harder This Time.*

It's not a huge deal that you revealed you stalk him. And hey, he keeps tabs on you too. You're just a couple of stalkers.

And damn, that stalker can kiss.

We're talking the weak-in-the-knees, flip-of-the-belly, tingles-down-the-arms style of smooching.

Just don't do it again.

Also, you're out of milk. Get some at the store, along with Cinnamon Life cereal. Sublimate with that. Tastes just as good as a hot kiss.

'Kay, thanks, bye. You're awesome, self.

6

At long last, Friday rolls around.

I'm as antsy as a feisty Chihuahua, a bundle of live wires all through the workday.

When the day ends, I close up and make a beeline for the gym for a quick workout. After I shower, I put on my best slacks and a freshly pressed shirt. Popping in earbuds, I play my lucky Sinatra playlist as I leave, walking among the Friday evening Manhattan crowd on my way to meet Doug at his favorite spot for dinner—Portnoy's, a tavern on the Upper East Side. As the crowd thins, I switch off "Strangers in the Night" and put in a call to my mother, who answers on the third ring.

"No, Cole. Leave it. Leave it on the deck. Leave it now."

She's talking to the dog. My mother is always talking to dogs. With a father who was a vet and a mom who took in strays, it's not as if I had a lot of choice in my profession. And that's just fine with me.

"Good boy. Good boy, Cole. You're so handsome. You're the most handsome boy I've ever known."

"What am I? Chopped liver?" I ask, managing to get a word in edgewise.

"You're my smart one," she answers diplomatically. Then her voice rises. "And you're the best boy, Porter. The absolute best."

Yup, we've got the handsome boy, the best boy, and the smart one. I have no illusions about the pack order. "It's a good thing I'm well adjusted, or I might resent your secret preference for dogs over your own son."

"Oh, please. Don't be silly. I don't harbor any secret favoritism of the pups." She pauses. "It's blatant."

"Indeed it is." I sidestep a throng of long-legged women huddled over phones as I head to the restaurant. "I'm off to my dinner now with Doug."

"Ooh, is that tonight?"

"He said he had big news about the practice to discuss, and he's been cutting back his hours in the last year. I even went ahead and prepped the paperwork. Just to get ahead of the game. Be ready, and all that."

"You were always two steps ahead on everything. That's wise, to be prepared."

"Exactly. As soon as we firm up the details, I can move forward with all the specifics."

"Your dad would be so proud. It's what he's always wanted for you. What he wanted for himself. And you're doing it." Her voice tightens, but just as quickly she softens. He's been gone long enough that the pain has lessened for her, for all of us. It's background pain. Present, but not too intense.

"I wouldn't have been able to do this without what he'd taught me . . . or without your support."

"Let me know how it goes. I'm sure it's going to be great," she says. "And get your butt out here to celebrate this weekend!"

"Love you, Mom. I'll catch the first train to Warwick in the morning."

I stuff the phone into my back pocket, turn into the restaurant, and say a quick prayer that this is the start of the next phase of my career. The one I've been wanting since I was still hitting high notes when I sang.

Doug is parked at the bar, his salt and pepper hair slicked back, nursing a gin and tonic.

He's twenty-five years my senior. The man who gave me my first big chance. I owe a ton to this guy. Doug, though he has his faults, has been impeccable at business. I respect the hell out of him. That's why I had to stay away from Sloane, even though I had no clue she was his daughter when I started seeing her. They don't have the same last name.

He stands, claps me on the back, and says hello, telling me the conference he just went to was *the best*. Everything is *the best* for Doug. He glances around the wood-paneled restaurant with high-backed red booths. "Want to know why I love this place so much?"

"Tell me."

"Because I never took any of my wives here." *Wives* being the operative word. He's had enough to need all the fingers on one hand to count.

"So it's the man zone, then," I say, peering around.

He smacks the bar for emphasis. "Not a single one of them," he says, as if proud of this accomplishment. "A man needs to keep some places sacrosanct from the women in his life. It wasn't easy, but I kept all four away."

I force out a laugh. "And how's it going with the fifth?"

"Helena's my favorite. She's the only one who's been here, but then, she's the keeper among the bunch. She's been instrumental in so many things."

"Such as?"

He signals for the tab. "We'll get to that. Let's get a table, Malone. I've done all my best deals here. This place and me—we're tight."

I smile deep inside my soul. May ours be the next great deal he inks here.

The hostess shows us to a booth near the back, tells Doug she'll transfer the tab, then hands us the wine list.

As he scans the offerings, Doug clears his throat. "How do you think things are going with the practice?

Did everything go well when I was at the conference this week?"

"Everything was great. We're running at top levels of efficiency and client care," I say, since that was one of my goals when he made me a junior partner—give our patients the time they deserve, but don't make the next appointment have to wait too long. "The staff is great. Jonathan and Sam are top-notch at moving the day along."

Could this conversation be going any better? This is clearly the start to the next chapter in our clinic.

"I couldn't agree more. And you've done an amazing job in seven years," he says, and the mention of the time frame is a sharp reminder of what started and ended seven years ago when I spotted the photo of Sloane on his desk at my job interview. When he told me, *Don't get any ideas.*

I wiped all ideas out of my head then.

The waiter pops by and asks if we want a drink.

"A bottle of your best cabernet sauvignon," Doug says with the kind of authority a silver fox can command.

Mentally, I pump a fist. Doug loves red. It's his celebration drink of choice. He always gets the best red to deliver the best news.

The waiter tells us he'll be right back, and Doug returns seamlessly to the conversation. "As I was saying, you've done a hell of a lot. Your father would be proud of you. You know that, right?"

"I do."

"And I want you to have all the things you've been working toward."

Damn, I won't be able to contain my excitement if it keeps on like this.

The waiter brings the wine and uncorks it. He pours a small amount into a fat glass. Doug picks it up and tastes, then declares it fantastic. The waiter pours some for me, sets down menus, and leaves.

Doug raises a glass. "Let's toast."

Fuck yeah.

I raise mine, waiting for him to make the next move.

He lifts his glass higher, and we clink. "To another year together."

All the air leaks out of me. "Excuse me?" I stumble on my words.

"Let's drink to one more year."

"Oh. Well. I thought you were retiring? You've cut back your hours significantly. You've been talking about retiring." *All the freaking time.*

"You're eager to see me go?" He arches one brow.

I shake my head quickly, needing to cover up any enthusiasm I might have shown. "No, I just thought, well, since you're not there as much, and you've been playing golf more . . ."

"There's plenty of life in this old dog. The ticker is strong." He taps his sternum. "Energizer Bunny and all. Must be all the horizontal activity I partake in. It's good cardio, you know. Keeps a man young and fit."

I groan inside. "I'm sure," I say, doing my best to present a cheery front.

"In any case, we've got another year together, and I'm confident this year will be the best one."

"Why's that?" I'm strangling on my own fucking shock. This is not how tonight was supposed to go.

"Because my daughter, Sloane, is going to be working with us."

7

Sloane Elizabeth's Voice Memo to Self on ARE YOU KIDDING ME?

Be cool.

Be calm.

The man is helping in the most amazing way.

Lord knows, you need it now. You need it for the cats and the dogs and your own damn dreams. He's making them possible.

Just walk into dinner like the strong, sharp, kick-ass woman you are. Be grateful, be humble, and don't let on to Daddy that you want to bang his business partner.

Darling Daddy would not like that for his sweet, innocent daughter.

Sigh. That's how daddies see their little girls.

You are so not innocent.

Not with the thoughts you've been having.

8

Perhaps I am dense.

Maybe I'm clueless.

Certainly, my ex-girlfriend Lucy tried to hang the clueless gold chain around my neck. The time she dragged me to Bed Bath & Beyond to shop for towels then asked which ones I liked for *our* apartment.

I'd flinched. "Our apartment? But we don't live together."

She'd rolled her eyes and flashed a knowing smile. "Why else did you think I wanted to take you towel shopping? You're so adorably clueless."

At that point, I picked up on her *clues* loud and clear, and nixed things before she made a copy of my key and moved in late at night while I was sleeping.

But this seems a little different than Lucy's off-hand comment. This seems like maybe, in retrospect, I might have jumped the gun.

Still, all the signs pointed to Doug telling me he

wanted me to take over the practice, not him telling me his gorgeous, smart, sexy daughter is evidently going into business with us.

Talk about whiplash.

He gestures toward the door. "I think you've met once or twice, and I invited Sloane to join us tonight."

I turn around, my heart squeezing with a myriad of *what the fuck do I do now* emotions as Sloane walks to our table as if on cue, looking as fascinating, as beautiful, as alluring as she did the night I met her seven years ago. I'd been singing karaoke at the fundraiser, and I'd nearly stopped in the middle of *Isn't It Romantic?*, jumped off the stage, and made sure she didn't leave. She stayed though, and it wasn't even her beauty that demanded my attention, though of course I noticed her face. It was something in her eyes. A sparkle, a glint. Something intriguing that said there was so much more to her than the surface, and I had to know what was beneath.

Every time I've seen her since, it's the same. The light's on her, only her.

Like it was the other night on the street when she kissed me.

My dick stirs at the memory. Well, dicks do like kisses. All kinds of kisses.

That's really fucking inconvenient—a semi when I need to stand up, say hello, and act like I don't want to do bad things to her.

Not as inconvenient, though, as the rug being pulled out from under me.

"Nice to see you again, Sloane," I say, stripping my voice to a monotone as I extend a hand.

She shakes. "Good to see you again too, Malone."

We're so business-like. I'm looking forward to receiving my Oscar for nonchalance.

"Your names rhyme," Doug remarks. "That's amusing."

"Yes, it sure is," I say, and honestly, isn't the rhyming names proof enough that nothing should ever happen with us? Sloane and Malone sounds dippy.

Doug rubs his hands together. "Let's dive into things, and then we can order. Sloane, why don't you start with what we discussed earlier today?"

She squares her shoulders. "It's always been my dream to save all the animals, so I started an animal rescue. It's been going well." She knocks on the table. "But you know how hard it is to stay afloat in that business. Well, I presume you do."

"I get it. It's tough," I say, since it's not an easy field to be in, but it's such a vital one.

Doug wraps an arm around his daughter's shoulders, and I wince a little bit at the reminder of who she is to him. Just, you know, his *offspring*.

"She's been running it from a little storefront in Brooklyn, and the rent is going up, and the landlord is terrible. I thought we could bring her in-house, and we'll handle all the spays and neuters. It'll come from my cut," he says, and he's thought of nearly everything.

And clearly this is *all* he's been thinking about discussing at dinner. Not my future hopes and dreams.

"I don't mind providing free spay and neuter," I say, still flummoxed that my expectations were knocked to their knees tonight. Wait, make that knocked to their ass.

"Nonsense. I'll take care of it. I insist. But I do hope you'll be okay with Sloane running the operation from my office," he continues. "It's all foster-based, with no animals kept on-site. They're all placed with volunteers who foster them till they're adopted, so it's not a question of space. I should have asked you first, but honestly, I was so damn excited."

He should have mentioned it to me, but he's still the senior partner. He started the practice years ago. He hired me as an employee seven years ago and brought me on as a junior partner three years later. But at the end of the day, he's still the big kahuna.

He still has more say.

But what was *her* say? Did she know about this plan the other night? Was her kiss designed to soften me up?

Well, it didn't work.

It made me hard instead. So there.

Doug shares more details then asks if this is all okay.

"Sure." What else can I say that doesn't make me sound like a supreme douche? Besides, I have to admit —it's a great idea for her rescue, and as someone whose father dreamed of going into business with his son once upon a time, I understand why he'd want this too.

Sloane smiles, and it's full of gratitude. Maybe relief too. "Thank you. I was so worried Best Friends wasn't going to make it. This gives us a shot in the arm for the next year, and I'm confident I can have everything built up and solid by then."

Doug lifts the bottle. "Why don't you have a glass of wine, and let's all toast together?"

She shakes him off. "You know I don't like red."

He arches an eyebrow. "You don't like red?"

"She prefers champagne," I cut in, and then I want to smack myself. How the hell would I know that from the occasional run-in with her? I only know it because of our time together.

Doug doesn't notice though.

"Let me get you some white instead." He flags down the waiter and asks for a glass of chardonnay.

The waiter brings it over, and the three of us raise our glasses. I take a hearty swallow. Hell, maybe I ought to get drunk tonight. Nothing makes disappointment go down quite like alcohol.

We peruse the menus quickly and place our order. When the waiter leaves, Doug remains eminently pleased.

"What could be better?" Doug asks, a satisfied grin on his face. "Can you think of anything better than this?"

"I can't," Sloane answers, and her smile matches

his, but I can detect hints of surprise and a little bit of discomfort in it. "I definitely can't think of anything better than this. I just didn't realize that you were going to have Malone here at dinner."

"Didn't I tell you?" Doug asks her, narrowing his brow.

"I'm pretty sure I would have remembered it." Her tone is light, but I get her meaning. "But then, I didn't even know about your idea till earlier today."

Ah, that must be for my benefit. She doesn't want me to think she knew about this when she kissed me.

Doug spreads his arms wide, like he's a magnanimous king. "I thought it'd be a great opportunity for all of us to get together and chat, see how we envision things working in the next year. My darling daughter," he says, dropping a kiss to her forehead. Then he gestures to me. "And you're practically a son."

Sloane jumps in like a leopard, so I don't have to. "He's not your son."

"And yet I care for Malone like he is," Doug says, looking at me with import in his eyes.

"And you know I've looked to you like a mentor," I say, emphasizing that word, because I don't think of him like a father, though I suspect he wishes I did. Just because my dad is gone, and has been since I was eighteen, doesn't mean I need a replacement. Doug's been my business go-to guy, and I'll forever be grateful for the role he's played.

"Regardless of what we call it, my two favorite people are here," Doug says, then downs the rest of his glass. "And now I must excuse myself to the little boys' room."

He exits, and the tension between Sloane and me tightens like a tourniquet.

I wish Sloane didn't look so delectable, wearing jeans and a simple white blouse. Her hair is swept up, revealing her neck, a neck that she loves having kissed.

Must wipe thoughts of her erogenous zones from my mind. Besides, I need to know something. I want to be certain she wasn't aware of her dad's plans the other night. "Did you know what he had in mind? When I saw you?"

Her eyes widen, and she shakes her head. "I didn't know he wanted to do this till this afternoon. It was a surprise to me. He gets an idea in his head, and he thinks he's doing it the best way, because he knows how much I need this. But I didn't know you were going to be here."

That's when something new and unpleasant occurs—the idea that she'd rather I not be here. "Is it a problem? Do you want me to leave?"

"No," she says in an instant. "We're going to be working together. We should be able to work together. I can try not to be around that often," she offers, "if it makes things easier."

"Why would it make things easier?"

"If things are awkward."

"Why would things be awkward? Because of Plant?"

Her brow creases. "Plant?"

I wave a hand dismissively. "Bumper. Salad. Petunia. The guy you were having dinner with the last time I saw you."

A laugh bursts out and she clutches her stomach. "Basil," she says, choking on the word as she laughs. "His name is Basil."

"Basil. Well, there you go. I was close."

"Basil is a good friend. He's a DJ. He's into music. You'd like him."

Doubtful.

"And you're staying with him?"

"No. Nor was I dating him." She stares at me like I'm a curiosity. "Are you jealous?"

I could play this one of two ways. Lying gets me nothing. The truth at least makes this night more . . . illuminating, and I'd really like some more light shed on this woman. "Yep. The full-on, one-hundred-percent, red-blooded kind."

She swallows. "That's interesting."

"And do you think that makes things awkward?"

She licks her lips. "It would be awkward if you were still seeing Clove."

It's my turn to knit my brow. "Who on earth is Clove?"

She crinkles her nose, a touch derisively. "Who knows? Whoever the latest woman is who falls at your feet when you sing."

I smile. "There's no Clove. No Jane. No Cindy. No Madison. There's no one."

"If there's no Basil and no Clove, why is there all this . . . tension?"

Checking the hall to make sure the coast is clear, I lean closer, my eyes locked on hers. "You know why there's tension."

"Why?" Her voice trembles.

Yup, the illumination is indeed growing brighter.

"Because you kissed the fuck out of me the other night, and because I'm still thinking about it. And because if your father wasn't in the bathroom, I'd kiss you even harder right now. So hard you'd see stars. You'd grab your purse and say, 'Let's get out of here right now.' Because you and I have unfinished business, and you know it."

She shudders, and a gust of breath seems to pass her lips. Her cheeks flush red, and I love, fucking love, the effect I have on her. Even though I shouldn't love it. I definitely shouldn't love it at all. But I do, and I love it more when her tone reveals the truth—it's breathy and hot as she says, "Is that how you'd kiss me? Like we have unfinished business?"

I lean back in the booth, never taking my eyes off her gorgeous face. "Sweetheart, you know exactly how I want to kiss you. You know exactly what we'd be capable of in bed."

Her shoulders rise and fall as she peeks behind her. We're alone still. Her voice goes softer. "If we were in an alternate universe right now, you could do all those things."

I groan audibly. This woman is going to make it so

damn difficult at work. "And maybe in some alternate universe we'd be in my building, the door falling shut, and you'd grab me and wrap your legs around me in the stairwell."

Her breath hitches, but she shakes her head. "I don't think so."

I tilt my head to the side. "That's not what would happen?"

The smooth sole of a shoe runs across my pant leg. She's playing footsie. "No, you'd toss me over your shoulder, carry me up the stairs, and take me against the door."

I grin wickedly. "And then on the counter."

"And then the couch," she adds. "Or wait, how about up against the window?"

"That can be arranged. I have floor-to-ceiling windows."

Her eyes dance with mischief. "And is there a view?"

"Of all of lower Manhattan, sweetheart," I say, and there is nothing awkward at all anymore.

"Take me to your parallel universe, please," she says.

I'm about to say *Let's get out of here now*, as if we're on a date, as if it's only the two of us.

And it hits me.

I'm doing it again.

I'm flirting with her.

Caught up in the vortex of Sloane Elizabeth. She's

a hurricane of sexuality, a storm of lust and desire, and I want to be caught in the eye.

"We should stop."

She blinks and squeezes her eyes shut, then opens them. "Yes, we should."

I have to be an adult. I have to be mature. I'm thirty-five years old, and I can't let hormones control my actions. Those days are behind me.

"Let's just agree that it was one kiss on the street, and it can't happen again."

"It definitely won't happen again."

Doug returns to the table, and I manage to be incredibly well-behaved for the rest of the evening. Tonight, I'm not simply the smart one. I'm the good one.

Even though I'll be thinking about that alternate universe later when I'm home alone in bed.

And probably tomorrow morning in the shower too.

And honestly, that'll be the trick to surviving having her in such close working quarters. For the next goddamn year of my life.

Water streams over my head. Images dance before my eyes. Yup, this is exactly what I need to recalibrate.

Steaming-hot water, a very active imagination, and that fantastic ability I happen to possess: being able to picture Sloane naked.

Sloane stepping into the shower.

Sloane wrapping a hand around my neck, tugging me close for a kiss.

Her hand sliding between our wet, slick bodies. Finding my dick, hard and aching for her.

A sly smile, a murmur, and that look in her eyes. The one that says *Let me get down on my knees.*

"If you insist," I'd say, and I jerk harder, stroke faster as Shower Sloane takes me in her mouth, brings me to the back of her throat, and wraps her lips so nice and tight around my shaft that my vision goes hazy. Pleasure barrels down my spine, rushing hot and fast. I'm there, over the edge, shuddering. I slam a palm against the tiled wall, cursing.

Hell, that came on faster than I expected.

Then again, in my defense, I was pretty damn pent-up.

But now I'm all good, and ready to tackle the year ahead.

9

My sister lands a devastating side snap kick that radiates through my bones. I counter it with an arm lock. She narrows her eyes, red billowing from the corners. I know that look.

She's a bull in the ring, dead set on charging me. But I also know how to deflect because I've been taking this Sunday night class for as long as she has.

We parry and spar for several more minutes until the session ends.

The instructor strides over and squeezes Truly's shoulder. "Well done. It's almost as if you two wanted to kill each other for real," Natalie jokes.

"You should see us when we get really mad," Truly says.

Natalie laughs. "I'll do my best not to incite your ire. But you guys are doing great." She taps her chin. "We have a tournament coming up. My kids are doing it. You guys should do it too."

Truly gives her a curious stare. "Are you saying you think I should fight your kids? Because I'm good, but I wouldn't want to run into your kids in a dark alley. They're tough."

"As they better be. They have been practicing martial arts since they could walk. But think about it." Natalie tightens her blonde ponytail. "After all, Jason is doing it," she says, mentioning my best friend.

Truly's navy eyes widen. "Jason's in the tournament?" Her voice pitches up the slightest bit.

"Do I detect a note of interest in the tournament now?" Natalie asks with a tilt of her head.

"I second that question," I say, raising my hand.

Truly scoffs, shaking her head. "My only interest is in kicking his butt. Speaking of, where is he tonight? Afraid of getting destroyed?"

"He's at a wedding," I answer. "But your interest in his whereabouts is duly noted."

"Oh, please. As if that's even a thing."

Natalie chuckles softly. "Interest or not, think about the tournament. You'd be great, Truly." She turns to me. "You'd be fine too, but I do want more awesome women showing up. Girl power and all."

"You are the poster child for girl power," Truly says admiringly, since Natalie teaches martial arts— she started in karate and moved to jujitsu recently— and also runs a construction business with her husband, one of our cousins.

"And on that note, this girl needs to get back out

there," Natalie says as the next class shuffles into the studio.

We leave, and I narrow my eyes, studying my sister. "So, tell me when this interest in my best friend began."

"On the fifth of never."

"You're in the full-blown denial stage. Got it."

"There's no denial. It was merely a curiosity since he's better at jujitsu than you, and I like to spar with people who make me stronger."

I ignore the dig, savoring the chance to needle her. "So it's safe to say it made you sad that he wasn't in class today?"

"Sad that I couldn't destroy him."

My sister took up jujitsu a few years ago, dragging me along and saying any self-respecting single woman in New York City needed to learn a martial art. I agreed wholeheartedly, and I enlisted Jason to join us. He's usually a Sunday night regular.

As we turn the corner onto Sixth Avenue, she shifts gears. "Are you ready for tomorrow?"

She knows the deal. I updated both Mom and Truly after the Friday night fiasco, otherwise known as My Big Lesson in Not Counting Chickens before They Hatch.

"I'm ready and eager for Sloane's first day. It'll be a walk in the park. A piece of cake. A cinch."

She shoots me a doubtful stare. "I'm going to give you a week till you cave. You do know you have high levels of manwhore in you?"

I scoff. "Please. I'm no manwhore. I'm picky. I'm like those people at the farmers market who take a long time with peaches, apricots, and apples."

She pats my cheek. "You're cute with your fruit euphemisms. Like I said, you're good for seven days. Wait. No. I'm being far too generous. Better make that a day."

"While I appreciate your unerring faith in me, it's unnecessary. I have a foolproof plan."

"Do tell."

"It's easy," I say as the sun dips in the sky. "I've been working on the necessary skills."

"And those are?"

I mime putting on a pair of shades. "I'm going to look at her through a professional lens only. The same way I look at Jonathan or at Sam. That's all there is to it."

"Well, that ought to be a piece of cake. Wait, no. A cinch. Actually, make it a picnic."

The trick is indeed about eyesight. It's about how you see things, how you approach the task at hand.

Focus is literally everything.

It's focus that got me through college with straight As. It's focus that saw me through veterinary school at the top of my class. It's focus that won me my first job, and it's focus that brought me to where I am now —well-respected, successful, and with clients who have a high regard for how I treat their four-legged family members.

Today, I must be the best at resisting an irresistible woman.

As I head into work, I say hello to Jonathan and Sam, breathing a sigh of relief that Sloane isn't in yet.

Jonathan and Sam give me eager *what happened* eyes.

"So? Am I making my special strawberry cupcakes with shots of frosting in the middle to celebrate?" Sam asks with a hopeful grin. "I baked them for my mom the other night, and even she liked them, and you know how picky that woman is."

"She is the nit-pickiest," Jonathan seconds, then stares at me, raising his thumb up then down, waiting.

They don't dislike Doug, but the reality is they're *my* people. I brought them on board, trained them, and worked closely with them to improve the practice. We have a rhythm to our day, an ease.

I sigh. "It's not happening yet," I say, then dive into a quick explanation of what went down.

"Does this mean Doug will be around more?" Sam sounds more concerned than I'd expected, maybe nervous too. "He was down to two days a week."

"He'll probably be here a little more often. Is that a problem?"

Sam gulps, shaking her head quickly. Too quickly. "No. It'll be fine."

I stare at her. "I don't believe you."

She glances around, making sure he's not here.

"It's just that . . . well, I started when he was cutting back. I hardly see him, and when I do, it's like running into the school principal. He's so much older, and serious. I don't know how to talk to him."

Laughing, I lean against the wall next to her desk. "Just talk to him like you talk to clients. You're great with clients."

"Because they're not the big boss!"

I tap my chest. "Hello! I'm your boss too. You talk to me just fine."

"Because you hired us," Jonathan puts in. "And despite your weird taste in music, you're mostly a cool guy."

"Gee, thanks. Also, old standards are not weird."

"They're kind of weird. But you know what I mean," he adds with a casual shrug. "You're easy to talk to."

"Plus, you say yes to things like pizza Fridays, and you give us movie tickets," Sam adds.

I blow on my fingers. "I am kind of amazing." Then I take a more serious tone. "It's going to be fine. I'll still be here, we'll keep working on our plans for the practice, and you can still ply me for movie gift certificates, and because I'm such a pushover, I'll probably keep saying yes."

Sam puts on a big, gleaming grin. "Cool. Can I also have a gift card for that new coffee house? Because they have awesome pour-overs."

"You're such a hipster," I say, shaking my head. "Also, Sloane is twenty-nine, so she's close to your age. I'm sure you can discuss your dubstep Scandinavian EMD music with her." I shudder at the thought of such tunes.

Sam pumps a fist. "Yes! Woman power!"

"Look, the bottom line is this: we want you to be ruler of this place someday," Jonathan says.

"And we'll keep working toward that," I say.

"And when you're in charge of everything, can you pay for me to go to vet school? Pretty please?" Jonathan takes a quick breath, like he's nervous to make this request.

But it's a no-brainer. That's exactly what my dad would do. I clap his shoulder. "If you stay on board, yes, I will do that."

His eyes turn to moon pies. "Shit. Are you for real?"

"Sure. You're damn good at this. I know you've been studying for vet school. It's a huge undertaking, but incredibly rewarding, and I believe you'd be a great vet."

"And you'd pay for it? Hell, I just threw that out there, just in case, but I didn't think you'd catch it."

I mime catching a ball. "Consider it caught." I turn to Sam. "Who have we got today?"

Sam hands me a chart, chuckling under her breath. "Janice Clarke is worried that her dog Ruby is, well . . . she has this toy monkey and . . ." Sam whispers the rest of it.

I nod. "Ah, got it."

Jonathan and I head into the exam room where

Janice is wringing her wrinkled hands and pursing her lips.

"Hey, Janice. How's our sweet Ruby-cakes today?" I ask, bending down to pet the wiggly dachshund mix.

"Oh, she's fine, Dr. Goodman. She's just fine. Except for one little thing."

"What's going on with Ruby?"

The woman's cheeks turn cotton-candy pink. "She likes to, um, well, she likes to . . ." Janice lowers her head, takes a deep breath.

I pet Ruby's back. "She has special feelings for this monkey? Is that it?"

Janice snaps up her gaze. "Yes! Exactly!"

I smile. "So you've got a dog who's overly affectionate with a stuffed toy."

"Yes," Janice says, cringing. "But, Doctor, she won't stop. She just keeps going at it. She drags the monkey off the shelf, she brings it to the bed, and she just, well, you know . . . for several minutes. She loves her stuffies. She sleeps with them, plays with them, even watches the washing machine when they go in there."

"Seems like Ruby's quite dedicated to her toys."

"But *why* is she engaging in this behavior with the monkey? She's a girl dog. I don't understand. Is she gender-confused?"

"That's not how it works, Janice. Canines are quite binary in their mating."

"And she's been fixed too!"

"Does she seem stressed or anxious?" I ask, and we briefly discuss and rule out other possible motives.

"Why is she doing this, then?" Janice asks.

"The same reason people do it."

"Do you mean . . .?" Her hand flies to her chest, and she whispers, "I don't hump a monkey."

"I don't either," Jonathan mouths, and I shoot him a side-eye glance.

"Your dog is masturbating," I tell Janice. "Since nothing seems wrong with her, she's likely doing it because it feels good."

A sheet of pure mortification slides over her face. "My dog is a pervert?"

I laugh, shaking my head. "No. She's normal. It's one hundred percent normal behavior. Both altered and intact dogs do it, and it's not limited to males. Females do it too, and many dogs also exhibit courtship behavior toward the stuffed animals, or whatever the object of affection is." I turn to Jonathan. "Perhaps you can explain what that is."

Jonathan clears his throat. "It's when the dog's tail goes up and her ears rotate backward. They may also lick and paw. Also, when they perform pretend bows. Play bows. That's all part of it."

Janice gasps. "She does all of that."

I clap her shoulder. "Then you have a very normal dog. If you don't like it, perhaps take the monkey away from her."

Janice shudders. "But she loves the monkey."

"Indeed she does."

Janice reaches for the small dog, scoops her up, and strokes her snout. "I just don't know what to do."

"It's certainly something to think about," Jonathan offers.

"Can we train her out of it?" Janice asks.

"If it's truly important to you, simply remove the temptation. However, Ruby might develop a liking for a favorite shirt of yours then. Sometimes it's best to just let dogs be dogs."

We say goodbye to Janice and move on to other appointments. I greet Doug when he arrives, and we cross paths all day long, as we usually do. I also see Sloane chatting on the phone in his office, tapping away on her computer, and keeping her head down. Her blonde hair is piled high on her head in a messy bun with soft tendrils framing her face.

I'm not tempted.

Not tempted in the least.

I wave and say hello.

She says hi back.

Look at that. Aren't we so damn cordial?

It's easy, too, as we review the paperwork on her current dogs in foster. A breeze as we discuss the shots they need. A picnic as we devise a plan.

It's all thanks to focus.

As the day draws to a close, Sam informs me that Lydia called, wanting to bring Sabrina in again. "This time, she's evidently hyper."

Jonathan shoots me an amused look as Sloane walks by. "That's the Doctor Doolarge effect."

Sloane stops in her tracks, arches a brow. "Doctor Doolarge?"

I groan.

Jonathan wiggles a brow. "Didn't you hear? He had his name changed."

I hold my hands up in surrender. "What am I going to do with you two clowns?" I say to Jonathan and Sam.

Sam shrugs. "I just don't know, Doctor Doolarge."

Sloane laughs as I head into the exam room for the last appointment of the day.

* * *

When I leave, I don't see Sloane anywhere. I tell myself to focus on finishing paperwork, but maybe I'll just poke my head into Doug's office.

I find him there at his desk. "Hey, Malone. How was everything today?"

"It was great."

"Not too disruptive having my girl here?"

"Not at all." That feels mostly true. We did get along well.

"We can start on the spay and neuters tomorrow."

"Sounds like a plan." I look around, as if Sloane is hiding behind a filing cabinet.

"Oh, she took off for the night. Said she had to go see a friend."

Friend.

This bothers me more than it should.

I slide my blinders back on as I work out, head to dinner with Jason, and then go home.

By the time I'm ready to hit the sack, my phone buzzes with a text from her that completely disrupts all my hard-won focus.

10

Sloane: Good evening, Doctor Doolarge. Wherever did the name come from?

Malone: I knew I would never live that down.

Sloane: So . . . do tell!

Malone: A client called me that.

Sloane: Were you involved with her?

Malone: No, but she was openly hitting on me in front of Jonathan.

Sloane: Your clients hit on you???

Malone: This surprises you? It shocks you into disbelief?

Sloane: I'm not shocked. I'm . . . annoyed.

Malone: Ah, the plot thickens.

Sloane: Did you go out with her?

Malone: What do you think?

Sloane: Just tell me.

Malone: Why are you asking?

Sloane: Humor me.

Malone: Fine. No, I did not. Are you happy?

Sloane: Yes. I'm glad you didn't go.

Malone: Your jealous side is adorable.

Sloane: I'm not jealous.

Malone: Maybe a little jealous?

Sloane: Just like you were jealous of Basil.

Malone: Completely jealous. Speaking of envy, is Basil the friend you're with tonight?

Sloane: No. I'm with Clove. His sister. :)

Malone: *rolls eyes*

Sloane: You deserve it. :) I went out with my friend Piper. She had a bad day, so I cheered her up with some Italian cookies and my upbeat attitude. She's the one I've been staying with, since she lives in Manhattan and it makes things easier with getting to the practice. Also, I found a foster home today for one of the dogs I picked up from another shelter!

Malone: That's fantastic news.

Sloane: What about you? How was your day? Any interesting cases?

Malone: I had a client who was worried about her dog masturbating on her toys and stuffies.

Sloane: Did you tell her everyone does it?

Malone: Everyone? Including you?

Sloane: Oh, c'mon. As if I don't.

Malone: Do you? Regularly?

Sloane: Do you?

Malone: This morning, as a matter of fact. And about an hour ago.

Sloane: You're quite a regular.

Malone: And you? Are you dodging the question, or is this a case of the lady never tells?

Sloane: I don't believe you asked a question.

Malone: Are you a regular?

Sloane: I am, but my toy of choice is a sleek silver dolphin.

Malone: Now that is a new image I'll have to bring into the photo album.

Sloane: I'm in your photo album?

Malone: You definitely play a role in my dirty dreams.

Sloane: Same here. Even though I didn't think of you naked at work. I need you to know that.

Malone: Not once?

Sloane: Fine. It crossed my mind once.

Malone: Only once?

Sloane: Isn't once enough?

Malone: Oh, sweetheart, once with me will never be enough.

Sloane: Cocky much?

Malone: Just cocky enough.

11

Even top athletes let their focus slide when they're off the court.

Can't fault myself for a few late-night text messages.

Fine, more than a few.

About a hundred. But I swear it was just harmless flirting, and it won't happen again.

Back to boot camp for me.

The next morning I work out at the gym with renewed vigor, I walk to the office with purpose in my stride, and I tackle the day with a sharpened eye.

I'm a fucking top-of-the-line Nikon.

Even though Sloane is in and out of the office, looking delectable as always, I am on point.

I'm an Olympic athlete, I'm a neurosurgeon, I'm an astronaut. Nothing about her distracts me.

Not that freaking pink shirt when it slopes off her shoulder.

Not the sweet vanilla smell of her skin when she reviews some of the foster dogs and their medical needs.

And definitely not the charming, bell-like laugh she emits when she and Sam debate which nearby coffee shop has better beans and cuter baristas.

I'm definitely not at all distracted when she pops into my office at lunchtime and hands me a Vietnamese noodle dish she says she picked up from a shop around the corner. What would distract me about noodles?

Certainly not when she says, "I remember you said Vietnamese had become your favorite cuisine."

My lips curve into a grin as memories streak by. Late-night walks, and dates, and explorations across the city. Dirty, flirty, naughty, wonderful, deep, and fantastic conversations that stretched late into the night. During that one delicious week, we were all about lingering talks, kisses on moonlit streets, and deliberate anticipation. We took things slow. We did it by choice, wanting to savor what had promised to be the sweetest, most tantalizing courtship. Like the time she told me she loved Vietnamese and I took her out to a restaurant I found, and after I told her it had become a favorite of mine too.

"Do you still like Vietnamese?" she asks.

I stand, walk around my desk, peek out the door. No one's nearby. She's inches away from me, and I take a step closer, stopping briefly to dip my face near her ear. "Yes. I very much do."

She shudders, and I'm a druggie. An addict, jacked up on his hit. One whiff of her sends my brain into overdrive, with wishes and wants crashing into each other.

"I should leave you with your noodles, then," she says, her voice breathy. Her body is radiating heat waves, and they're setting my skin on fire.

"Yes. You probably should, but I'm also excellent at sharing."

Her brown eyes are wide and hungry. "I like Vietnamese food too."

I gesture to the noodle dish. "We can talk about the no-hump Wednesday. Fitting, no?"

Her enticing lips tip into a grin. "So fitting."

She sits across from me, and we share a quick meal as we discuss the spay and neuter parade for tomorrow, and this almost feels like something that could have happened seven years ago.

What would have happened if I hadn't lowered the guillotine on our burgeoning romance?

The rest of the afternoon, I'm nose to the grindstone, seeing patients until the end of the day. Sam tells me our last appointment canceled.

I check my watch. Ten minutes till closing time. "Want to cut out early?"

She punches the air. "Yes!" Then she rearranges her features. "Just kidding. I want to stay and do extra work all night." Her smile is sweet and saccharine.

"Get out of here. I know that's a fib."

As she and Jonathan pack up to leave, the door bursts open and Sloane rushes in, clutching a tiny, trembling dog with big butterfly ears.

"I pulled him from animal control's shelter just now," Sloane says, adrenaline coloring her tone.

"Oh my God, he's adorable," Sam coos, racing over to the Papillon mix in Sloane's arms.

"He's so sweet too," Sloane says.

"Why don't you bring him into exam room one? I'll make sure he's okay," I offer.

"Thank you. The shelter said he was fine, no heart-worm, no visible issues. But I'd love for you to check."

I head into the room, and both women follow with Jonathan close behind.

"It's a dog party," Jonathan says, in a singsong voice.

The copper-colored mutt with white paws and the biggest doe eyes I've ever seen burrows deeper into Sloane's chest, tucking his snout underneath her arm.

Sam pets his back. "He's scared. He must have had a crazy day. How did you spring him?"

"He's so sweet, but he was sitting in the corner of the kennel just trembling and looking so frightened and pathetic. I couldn't resist."

"Who could resist those eyes? Even my mom wouldn't be able to turn you away," Sam says, encouraging the little fellow to poke his head out. Soon enough, the pup does, and somehow I manage the task of examining him while Sloane cradles him against her breasts, and my two employees watch.

Yup, this is platinum-level good-boy behavior now. I'm earning my medal tonight.

"What's his story?" I listen to his heart rate.

"He was living on the street. Picked up by animal control a couple days ago. He only had one night left," she says, while I check his teeth, "but I know we're going to find him a great home." She drops a kiss to his head, and it is one of the sweetest things I've ever seen. "You're going to be okay, Mr. Fox. I know you didn't like living on the street. I'm going to find such a good home for you, and it's going to be wonderful. You're going to find a person who loves you. I promise."

She gives him another kiss.

And fuck my focus.

My heart is thumping hard, and I want to wrap my arms around her, kiss her neck, and tell her the little guy will be okay. "Mr. Fox?"

"Well, he looks like a little red fox," Jonathan says.

"He totally does," Sam chimes in, and it's a damn good thing the two of them are here. If they weren't, I'd have to call my sister and tell her I was ready to cave in two days.

I'm such a sucker for a woman who's good with animals.

"Do you have a foster home for him yet?" I ask.

Sloane shakes her head. "No. I'm going to keep him with me tonight."

My heart softens even more. "Let me send you home with some food for him. And I'll call you a cab."

She snuggles him closer. "Thank you. I'd appreciate that."

A few minutes later, I put her, some cans of food, and Mr. Fox in a cab, wishing I was going with them too.

12

The next day is no-hump Wednesday, and the surgery lineup calls for a steady stream of snippety snip snips, both for patients and fosters.

I make my way through the alterations with sharp intensity, moving methodically and precisely through each one. Over lunch, my partner and I grab a quick bite at a nearby burger joint, discussing some of the more unusual ongoing cases I've been treating.

He's aces when it comes to obscure and off-the-beaten-path maladies. We tackle a case of a poodle with some vision issues, and Doug suggests a treatment he heard about at the last conference he attended. When the meal is done, he taps his temple. "See? I've still got it going on."

"You absolutely do. There's no one better."

We return to the office, and when he pushes open the door, he says offhand, "But someday soon, I'd like to retire. I have visions of playing golf and enjoying some salsa dancing with my favorite wife. Hell, maybe Sloane can give me grandchildren so I can enjoy them between tropical vacations."

I cough so loudly and virulently, it turns into a bark.

"Let me get you some water," Doug offers.

I wave him off. "I'm fine," I choke out.

But really, I'm not. The thought of her having children is too much because that would require another man to win her heart.

And to fuck her.

The thought of either of those things is like an obnoxious song, grating as it loops in my head.

* * *

Sloane's out for most of the day, but after lunch, she pops in my office wearing a huge grin. "Knock, knock?"

"Who's there?"

She points to herself. "The most kick-ass dog rescuer in the city. I found a foster for Mr. Fox. She picked him up this morning, and she's already sent me a few dozen photos of him for the rescue's website. Check it out."

She struts over to my desk and shows me the shots of the Papillion making himself at home. "One, you're awesome. Two, he's adorable. He looks like a Muppet."

She beams. "That's what I was saying earlier too."

As she leaves, I flash back to the conversation with Doug from lunch. Yup, the prospect of her with someone else hits all kinds of wrong notes.

* * *

As the workday winds to its end, I stroll through the cages for the post-op visits, checking out the kitties and pups we spayed today. All are doing well, and I make my final stop at an orange kitten who hangs his head low.

"Hey, Apricat. You doing okay?"

Meow.

"You're a little woozy," I say as the kitty stumbles toward the cage door.

Another abject mewl falls from his lips. After unlocking the cage, I scoop up the little dude.

"You're just a little lighter, Apricat. It's like you went to the seamstress and had your birthday suit tailored. You're going to be fine in no time."

The sweet little guy rubs his head against me, a purr daring to escape from his chest.

"That's right. Your foster is on her way. You'll go home in a few more minutes, just like the song."

I lower my voice, singing to the forlorn feline. *"When you're gone, I'm worried all day long. Baby won't you please come home."*

"Something you just make up on the spot?"

I turn around. Sloane's leaning against the wall, grinning. Has she been watching the whole time?

"Because that first line especially sounded vaguely familiar," she continues.

And that'd be a yes.

"It's 'Baby Won't You Please Come Home.' Charles Warfield and Clarence Williams. 1919. A very oldie, but very goodie. Ella Fitzgerald covered it. So did Sam Cooke and a lot of others."

"I bet that makes all the kitties swoon." Her grin is borderline flirty, telling me she enjoyed the impromptu show.

Still, I play it cool, like I'm not a total softie, even though she's clearly figuring that out. "I've been known to make a cat purr with my pipes."

"So you sing to the cats?"

Be tough. Be a lion. You're a badass alpha male.

"I can soothe even the most ferocious feline," I say like a play-brag even though it's the whole truth and nothing but.

"He can. And he does. I caught it on camera," Jonathan says as he pokes his head around the corner.

I sigh as I pet the kitty's chin. "You went *Candid Camera*?"

"Oh, c'mon. You've been singing to the cats for years, Dr. Goodman. This isn't the first time I've got it on video. It's too cute not to capture."

"Do you have a secret stash of videos of me?"

"Yeah, a private collection," he jokes. "How will I ever bribe you someday if I don't have them?"

Sloane glances at Jonathan, and a seed of an idea seems to cross her features. "Since Apricat is one of the rescue's cats, could I post that clip on our feed? It would help him get adopted," she says, dangling that little nugget before me.

"You so have to," Jonathan says, nudging me but keeping his eyes on Sloane. "I hereby grant you permission."

I pat my chest. "Hello? Isn't the permission *mine* to grant?"

Jonathan waves me off. "You're singing old standards to a cat. It's not like you're singing Panic! at the Disco. I feel like that's the permission slip."

I laugh and gently scoot Apricat back into his cage. "Fine, go ahead. It's not like it's going to ruin my street cred or anything."

"That's right." Jonathan makes his way toward the front desk, calling back, "You'd have to have some first for that to happen."

* * *

The fat white ball soars over the field majestically, rising higher until it drops into the great beyond. I pump a fist, and my teammates holler from the bench as I round the bases in the softball game that happens to fall on a Friday evening this week. As I cross the plate, my buddy Jason is waiting with a high five, and so is my cousin Nick.

"It's about time," Nick remarks, smacking my palm.

"If memory serves, I hit a homer the other week too."

"Eventually you'll learn to knock home runs in every single game, like I do."

He's not wrong. Nick Hammer is pretty much the gold standard when it comes to home runs, but I think I'm pretty damn close.

Jason scoffs. "What's truly impressive is when a lad from the mean streets of London can knock 'em all in. And I do my fair bit occasionally."

I laugh as we head to our bench. "Pretty sure you weren't exactly raised in the slums of your nation's capital."

"I had a right rough time."

"You're from freaking Notting Hill."

Jason scoffs. "Please don't let that load of crap get around. I was raised on the wrong side of the river. All that street fighting I had to do toughened me up."

"Wait." The pieces clicked and the light dawned. "This is one of your backstories, isn't it?"

"Maybe it is. Maybe it isn't." Jason has a closetful of identities, and he wears different ones for his job.

"Well, if it's true, it's a wonder you're not better at jujitsu, then," I say then point at Nick. "Speaking of, did you hear his sister-in-law wants you to do a tournament?" Nick's brother, also my cousin of course, is married to Natalie.

"She mentioned it. But I'm usually booked on weekends," Jason says.

Nick raises an imaginary violin and speaks in an imitation of Jason's British accent. "Woe is me, lads. It's so rough being a secret operative at fancy weddings, where I pick up women every single Saturday night."

"It's a tough job, no doubt, but someone has to be a best man for hire," Jason quips as the three of us head back to the field.

When the game ends, we head out of the park, chatting about work as we go, catching up on the TV shows Nick helms. The man is a wildly successful cartoonist who's created several successful late-night animated TV shows.

Nick smacks his forehead. "I almost forgot. I posted that video of you on my show's Facebook page and Instagram feed."

"One of me at Gin Joint?" I try to remember when Truly last shot a video.

"No. The one of you singing to the orange cat."

"Oh yes, wasn't that the dog's bollocks? Your sister sent it to us so we could have a laugh," Jason says.

"Thanks. Glad you enjoyed it. Be sure to tip the barkeep on the way out."

"Anyway," Nick interjects as we turn onto Fifth Avenue, "I called it *The Singing Vet*. And it did crazy well. Tons of views and shares."

I furrow my brow. That was the last thing I expected him to say. "It's odd sometimes, what people want to watch online."

Jason strokes his stubbled jaw as if deep in

thought. "It is bizarre, especially considering the obvious issue."

"What's that?" Nick asks.

Jason shrugs helplessly. "The fact that Malone's so damn ugly."

"Yeah, that's true." Nick sighs heavily. "I guess I can't cast you in a new web series called *The Singing Vet.*"

"It's okay. I understand how jealousy works. It's hard for both of you to be around such a supreme specimen," I say with a wink.

"And a humble one too," Jason adds.

"Just like you."

Nick pushes his glasses up the slope of his nose. "Seriously, though, the video did well. It doesn't hurt that there's a hot woman in it. The one who talks to you about the song."

A Pavlovian reaction kicks in at the mention of Sloane. My senses heighten. My mouth waters. And my brain slides an image of her front and center. "That's Sloane."

Nick snaps his fingers. "Yeah, the camera loves her. I mentioned her rescue when I posted it. Who knows? Maybe it'll raise some awareness for your practice and her rescue."

When Sloane texts me later that evening, I learn it's done more than raise awareness.

13

Sloane: HAVE YOU SEEN THIS?

Sloane: HOLY SOCIAL MEDIA!

Sloane: IS THIS POST EVEN REAL? AM I DREAM-ING? IF I AM, DON'T WAKE ME UP.

Sloane: THIS IS LIKE FINDING OUT I CAN RENT A ONE-BEDROOM IN THE CITY FOR $1000 A MONTH!

Malone: Don't be silly. You know a one-bedroom in the city for 1K is nothing but a fairy tale. That's like believing in Santa Claus.

Sloane: There's no such thing as Santa?

Malone: Hate to break it to you.

Sloane: Next thing I know you'll be telling me the sun doesn't rotate around Earth.

Malone: I'm a regular dream-crusher.

Sloane: You're actually a dream-maker. My rescue snagged nearly $5000 in donations tonight alone. From that video!!! I am over the moon!

Malone: That's amazing. You deserve it.

Sloane: I'm so happy, I could kiss your friend for sharing this.

Malone: Sorry, I must have heard you wrong. You said you could kiss Nick, but I think you meant to say you could kiss me.

Sloane: I CAN TOTALLY KISS YOU.

Malone: I'm heading to a gig in a few minutes. If you want to show up in the front row and then lay one on me, I'll be the guy holding the mic, wearing a tailored suit, singing love songs in my delicious crooner's tenor. (Hey, that's how the reviewer at *The City Observer* described me, just saying.)

Sloane: Don't tempt me.

Malone: Are you tempted?

Sloane: It's like you've dangled Peanut Butter Dream ice cream in front of me.

Malone: Take a lick. Hell, lick the whole damn cone.

Sloane: How did we get back to flirting so quickly? We were talking about the donations! The big, huge, awesome donations that I will put to excellent use.

Malone: We returned to flirting because you said you wanted to lick me. I can't help it if that's where your mind goes. Evidently, I'm lickable.

Sloane: So I should come listen and then lick you?

Malone: Brilliant idea!

Sloane: But seriously.

Malone: Why would you think I wasn't serious? I take you licking my cone incredibly seriously.

Sloane: Has anyone ever told you that you can turn anything into a dirty comment?

Malone: This from the woman who used two size-centric adjectives to describe a donation.

Sloane: I was talking about a monetary contribution!

Malone: Or maybe your mind is on all things big and huge.

Sloane: Like I said, you can turn everything naughty.

Malone: It's one of my great skills.

Sloane: You have many great skills.

Malone: That is true. But I won't be much use at the singing one if I'm late. I'll simply pretend you're in the front row and I'm singing to you to celebrate the BIG, HUGE, AWESOME . . . donation.

Sloane: You want me to come by and celebrate?

Malone: Let's be honest. A big, huge donation is celebration-worthy. We need to toast to it.

Sloane: Don't you think that would be dangerous though? As in tempting?

Malone: We lasted a week together in the office and didn't maul each other. Clearly, we're 100 percent in the friend zone.

Sloane: Is that so? A minute ago you asked me to lick you.

Malone: And now I'm cured. I see you as an undangerous, untempting, completely un-risky colleague. :)

Sloane: It's the same for me. I suppose, then, as an untemptress, I could come see you.

Malone: Now you're talking. And with you as an un-vixen, we can celebrate.

Sloane: Is anyone else going?

Malone: Hopefully everyone in New York. I enjoy a packed house. But if you're asking if you can have me to yourself to celebrate, the answer is yes. Seems fitting, since you were the one who encouraged me to go the Michael Bublé route.

Sloane: True. And you encouraged me to start a rescue.

Malone: And here we are, thanks to each other. Seems we have double to celebrate.

Sloane: I am grateful, Malone. No joking, no teasing. I am so grateful for your encouragement years ago.

Malone: I am too, Sloane. So much.

Sloane: One drink sounds lovely.

Malone: I promise I won't let you kiss me again, even if you try.

Sloane: Please. I can resist you.

Malone: Of course you can.

Sloane: You don't think I'm able to?

Malone: Just teasing. I have utter faith in your abilities. So much so that I'm not afraid to sing my sexiest, swooniest numbers in front of you tonight.

14

Sloane Elizabeth's Voice Memo to Self on Ten Things You Must Remember Tonight

1. One drink only.

2. No flirting. Absolutely no flirting.

3. Especially not if Malone is panty-meltingly gorgeous and sexy when he sings. Like he was that night he sang "Isn't It Romantic?" doing karaoke, and you pretty much turned into a puddle of liquid silver lust on the floor.

4. Wear something sensible so you don't feel sexy. Like a paper bag, a burlap sack, or a sumo wrestler costume. All of these are acceptable outfits. Please also consider wearing a pair of onesie pajamas,

because there is literally nothing less sexy on the entire planet than giant footsie pajamas on an adult.

5. Also, perhaps slippers?

6. Don't shave legs or armpits. That's basically anti-sex armor right there.

7. If all else fails, just think of Dad. Remember how he would feel if he knew.

8. *Shudder. Cringe.* Just erase all mention of that person from your head right now.

9. Remember you made it through the first week of working with the hot vet, and you can do anything.

10. But he's also a hot singing vet who's clever, sexy, and charming. How the hell are you going to pull this off? Text Piper. Even if she's out of town for the evening, clearly you need her reinforcement.

Piper: Hey, sexy lady!

Sloane: Wait. Do I look sexy?

Piper: You always look sexy, even though . . . what exactly are you wearing in that photo? Ohh! Is that a

black turtleneck? Are you channeling the ghost of
Steve Jobs? Because stop. Just stop.

Sloane: I'm going to see Malone play at Gin Joint, and
I'm trying to be unappealing.

Piper: Ohhhhhhhhhh.

Sloane: What was that ohhhhhhhhhh for? That it's
working—my unattracti-fying—or something else?

Piper: Gee. I don't know. What do you think it
was for?

Sloane: I'll be good! I've seen him for the last week,
and it's been completely fine. It's not like my heart
flutters wildly when I see him. It's not like my brain
flips back in time and remembers how it was. It's not
like he is as sweet and funny and flirty and sexy as he
was the very first night I met him.

Piper: So it's super easy? And in fact, the socks you
made to recognize your accomplishment really do
ring true? By the way, I bought them for a few clients,
as well as myself.

Sloane: What was the slogan again?

Piper: *My hands are tired from patting myself on the back.*

Sloane: Ha! That's right. So true.

Piper: So you patted yourself on the back for one week. And now you're going to see him sing. Question: do you want your ovaries to explode tonight?

Sloane: Question: why do people say "exploding ovaries" at all? That sounds incredibly painful. It doesn't sound positive.

Piper: Now is not the time for dissecting a popular saying. I only asked because I know what his voice does to you.

Sloane: It melts me.

Piper: Everything about him melts you. Remember how you felt way back when?

Sloane: Yes. Like I was falling in love.

Piper: And remember, too, how you felt when he ended it.

Sloane: But it had to end.

Piper: I don't dispute that. I just encourage you to remember how much it hurt when it did.

Sloane: Like a sledgehammer. Hey, have I ever told you you're nothing if not practical?

Piper: I have to be. I have to look out for the people I love. And I'm looking out for your heart. Plus, you still have The Thing to deal with.

Sloane: Don't remind me of The Thing.

Piper: I just want The Thing to be fixed. Hey, maybe he can fix The Thing! Why didn't we think of that?

Sloane: And I thought you were trying to keep me on the straight and narrow.

Piper: I was, till I thought about the possibility of reversing The Thing.

Sloane: I'm going to throw this turtleneck at you right now.

Piper: Good, then hopefully you won't wear it tonight. For the love of fashion, please change.

Sloane: That's a promise.

15

I never aspired to be a rock star, a crooner, or a Broadway belter.

I certainly didn't have it on my vision board to be a lounge singer. (If I had a vision board, which I don't and have never had.)

Singing was one of those things that I discovered I could simply *do*, though I never *did* anything with it. Growing up, there was no glee club, band, or a cappella group for me.

I started singing out of necessity.

Like many who came before me and many who will come after, I was *forced* to play the piano by my parents.

There was no love at first note. More like loathing.

I wanted to play sports, throw a ball, run across a field. But twice a week, I *had* to sit down and play. During one lesson my mother suggested I sing along to make the songs that—as I'd put it—*bored me to tears* more interesting.

The words somehow unlocked the music, and suddenly, piano was fun. It was a game I was good at. A chance, frankly, to show off.

Once I realized I could do it, singing was like juggling. It was a party trick. I was the guy who could nail "Happy Birthday" at a group dinner, I was a pro at "Take Me Out to the Ball Game" at Yankee Stadium, and when Christmas rolled around and you needed someone to belt out "Deck the Halls," I was your guy.

Then Sloane came around. She cheered the loudest when I sang karaoke at the charity event the night we met.

Later, during one of our dates, she said, "You should just do it. You have the voice for it. Go sing at a club."

I laughed it off. I had no aspirations to be Michael Bublé, thank you very much.

"But you don't have to make money at it," she'd said. "You don't have to make albums. You could just make music for fun. Think about it. Do it because it's something that you enjoy. Do it because it's an adventure."

Her idea weaved its way under my skin as she encouraged me.

"You have a real passion and a real gift. Don't let it pass you by. Singing doesn't have to be everything. But maybe it can be just enough to be your adventure."

She was right. It has been a fantastic journey. And for the first time since that fateful night I met her, I'm singing with her in the house.

All I have to do is remember she's not mine.

She can't be mine.

None of the obstacles between us have vanished. Her father is still my business partner. He's absolutely my mentor.

In fact, the hurdles are stacked even higher now that Sloane and I are working in the same damn space every day.

But tonight, we're here.

Gin Joint feels about as far away from the clinic as North Dakota is to Tahiti.

Tonight is for Tahiti.

I'm not nervous. I'm fired up when she walks in at the start of my set looking so damn blonde. Her golden hair cascades down her back and curls over her shoulders in soft waves. Her little black dress hugs her hips, and the silver pendant resting against her pale skin draws my eyes to her chest.

But her eyes lure me in.

They always have. They did that night I met her at a fundraiser for several local shelters. This was long before she'd started hers, back when she'd just finished her bachelor's degree and was trying to figure out what to do next.

I was already a vet, searching for a new job. We connected in an instant when I sang, and I knew I had to meet the gorgeous blonde in the front row.

As soon as I stepped off the stage, I made a beeline to her.

We shared a drink, then we shared a night.

Our connection was instant and intense, and more than physical attraction. I hadn't experienced that type of electric chemistry before, and even though I wanted her beneath me in my bed, I also enjoyed spending time with her. Her wit, her charm, her confidence—they hooked me. She was younger than I was. Twenty-two to my twenty-eight, and while that's not a big difference, neither was it the reason I took it slow. There was something worth slowing down for with her.

Until the day I walked into a job interview and spotted a framed photo of her on the desk.

When I told her we had to end it, her eyes filled with sadness.

Now, tonight, those deep brown depths are filled with an intensity that's so damn enticing as she watches me sing a Sinatra tune, since there's nothing better to open an act with.

When I finish my first number, I dive into a brief chat with the audience, as I often do.

"Ever invite a girl to an event? A woman who you've maybe had your eye on? Maybe for a while. Possibly for a long time?"

A couple of guys in the front row nod. They get

me. The sliver of a knowing smile sneaking across Sloane's face tells me, too, that we both know the score. We're both aware that we've stolen a moment tonight. That we've tangoed around each other all week, and we made our own loophole—one drink to celebrate.

Tonight is a bubble, and I'm going to enjoy the hell out of it until it pops. Because it will.

But for now, we're in an alternate universe. And in this world, you bet your ass I'm going to let the woman know that I fucking love singing to her.

I make my way back to the piano. "And then she shows up. As soon as you see her, as soon as your eyes meet hers, you're grinning. Because she's here. Because she made it."

I scan the audience, and now those guys are nodding. In her seat at a table in the front, the woman in question keeps her eyes on me. "Then you meet her gaze. And all you can think is 'Doesn't she look wonderful tonight?'"

A few women in the audience sigh contentedly. A couple of the guys look at their dates. Sloane glances down then back up, a grin tugging at her lips. When her eyes meet mine once more, I finish. "And then you understand a song completely."

I launch into one of the greatest love songs of all time, and when I'm done with "Wonderful Tonight," I can feel the energy vibrating from the crowd. It's electric and palpable. It's hot and bothered. A hum seems to radiate through the audience. Maybe everyone here is getting lucky tonight. Maybe everyone looks wonderful.

I ride that high, making my way through the rest of my tunes, sliding from Dean Martin to Tony Bennett, from Chris Isaak to Sam Cooke.

The more I sing, the more charged I feel.

My skin is buzzing; my bones are humming. I've been plugged in, and now I'm lit up from the music and the woman and the crowd. It's a perfect storm of energy and electricity, and we're feeding off of each other. Soon it's time to finish the act with "I Ain't Got Nobody."

"Won't somebody come and take a chance with me? I'll sing you love songs, honey, all the time."

When I'm done, I understand the words on another level.

Take a chance.

I haven't figured out how to jump over those hurdles that still exist. I don't know that I will anytime soon.

Sloane is off-limits, and probably always will be.

But I also know from her body language and her laughter that neither of us came here tonight for just one drink.

I thank the crowd and head straight to the woman who came for me.

16

Sloane Elizabeth's Mental Voice Memo to Self on Things to Research when You Get Home

- Look up if it's possible to overdose on swooning.
- Find out if other women have survived that song being sung to them, or if the objects of said singing are all now melted puddles.
- Perhaps they're being studied in a lab, to better understand the full scope of swoonitus.
- Note: research whether there is any swoonier song in the history of music than "Wonderful Tonight."
- Wait. No need to. There is obviously nothing else that can cause swoon overload like that tune.

- And now you're suffering from it big time, and there's no cure.

17

I guide her to the bar, my hand on her lower back, since I've discovered her dress is better than an all-expenses-paid tropical vacation.

It's the kind that has an open back.

I'd like to thank the inventor of this style. He or she deserves a Nobel Prize. Sloane's back is perfection. Smooth, soft, pale skin, and all of it is exposed for a visual feast.

Maybe I *am* in Tahiti tonight.

Maybe that's where my alternate universe exists.

"What did you think of the show?" I ask when we reach the bar.

A hint of a smirk tugs at her lips. "I think that you have a tremendously unfair advantage in life."

I furrow my brow as I rest an elbow on the bar's metal surface. "How so?"

She sets her hand on my arm and drags her fingers down the fabric of my suit jacket. That feels so much better than should be legal, even through the material. "You can't be this good-looking, this smart, this caring, this charming, and this talented too," she says softly.

I tap my chin. "Hmm. You're right. Something must be terribly wrong with me. Perhaps you'll find it."

"Mark my words: I'm going to figure it out. I'm going to get to the bottom of this. Because there's no way you landed all these panty-melting attributes without having terrible manners or bad breath or a closed mind."

I flash her a smile. "You're looking at a man who opens doors and says please and thank you, and my breath is minty fresh." I lean in closer. "Also, my mind is all the way open. To just about anything."

She gasps. Quickly, though, she seems to collect herself. "There has to be something." She scans me up and down with an imaginary flaw detector, like that will find it.

"I can't garden for shit," I offer.

She rolls her eyes. "That doesn't count."

I look up at the ceiling as if lost in thought. "My handwriting is wretched."

"Nope. Not enough."

"Fine. Sometimes I like to watch football on Sundays and do nothing else."

A hint of triumph crosses her eyes. "And do you do it in your boxers, occasionally scratching your balls?"

I scoff. "Please. No." I take a deep breath. "I wear lounge pants."

Her eyes light up. They absolutely dance in victory as she pokes my chest. "That's it. That's something I can work with. I can't stand lounge pants or sports."

"Or ball scratching?"

"Add them all together, and I've clearly located your flaw. Whew."

"We can hunt for other flaws if you'd like. I'm sure I have tons of terrible habits."

"Yes. Something has to be horribly wrong with you," she insists.

"What's wrong with him?" My sister jumps in, having just marched over to us. "Pull up a chair, honey. I hope you have all night though."

I roll my eyes, gesturing toward the brunette behind the bar. "Sloane, this is my sister, Truly."

Truly extends a hand to Sloane. "And you must be the famous Sloane Elizabeth."

"I'm famous?" Sloane looks to me with curious eyes, then back at my sister. "Nice to meet you."

"Good to meet you, and you are absolutely famous. He won't stop talking about you."

I glance at my twin. "Thanks, Truly," I say drily.

She shrugs, grabbing some napkins to stuff into a holder. "That's what sisters are for." She tips her head to Sloane. "What can I get you?"

"A glass of champagne."

Instantly, I wonder how the drink will taste on Sloane's lips.

"And a Scotch for you, I presume?" Truly asks me.

"Sounds great."

As Truly grabs the bottles, Sloane drums her fingers on the bar. Her nails are unpolished, and I love this detail about her. She's a woman who works with her hands, and high-maintenance polish wouldn't work for her. "Inquiring minds want to know. What did you tell her about me?"

"I might have mentioned you way back when."

"And what did you mention?"

"Oh, you know. Met a girl. She's fantastic. I can't stop thinking about her."

"Really?" Her lips twitch in a smile.

"Yes, really."

"I like that you told her."

The way she looks at me, the way she says those words, sends a charge through my body. It makes the rest of the club disappear. "Why do you like that?"

She inches closer. "I did the same. I told my friend Piper."

I arch an eyebrow, liking this information. "And what did you tell her?"

She runs her finger along the edge of the bar. "There was this guy . . ."

"And?"

Sloane shakes her head, her eyes a little nostalgic, her tone dipping into wistful. "You know what happened."

I sigh. "I do know what happened. And I told my sister that too. I told her how devastated I was when I went into your dad's office for my second job interview and saw the picture of you on his desk. Such a slap-in-the-face way to learn the woman I wanted was off-limits." I pause, exhaling heavily. "And still is."

She frowns. "Yes. So maybe we've found it."

"Found what?"

"The flaw," she says sadly. "I'm your business partner's daughter, and that's not changing."

"And your dad has made it clear on more than one occasion that you're off-limits."

"No one's good enough for his daughter, he believes."

"He definitely believes that. And to top it off, you're kind of, sort of my business partner in a way too."

She shoots me a look. "Great. Thanks for reminding me."

I smile. "What was I thinking? We're supposed to be celebrating your big, huge donation. Screw all this sad shit."

"Exactly. Tonight isn't about the past and what might have been."

Truly returns with our drinks, sliding a champagne to Sloane then a Scotch to me before walking away.

I raise a glass, and Sloane does the same. "To new opportunities," I offer. "And making sure you don't try to kiss me tonight."

She clinks her glass to mine, laughing. "I'll toast to making sure you don't try to kiss me. So there."

"Then let's drink to being friends."

"We can definitely be friends." She knocks back some of her champagne. "To celebrations. To friendships. To new times."

Unable to resist, I lean a little closer, getting a contact high from being inches away from her. "I like the sound of that very much."

A throat clears. A voice cuts through the heat we're radiating. "You guys should just get a room."

I point my thumb at my sister. "Ignore her. It's what I've done my entire life."

"Please. You've never ignored me," Truly says, parking her hands on the bar. "That's the problem. I'm that little voice on your shoulder."

Sloane meets Truly's gaze. "I'm glad you're his sister. I think he needs someone like you to keep him in line." Sloane turns to me, satisfaction in the set of her jaw. "Because I've figured out your flaw."

"What's that?"

Her irises twinkle with mischief. "You don't always listen to that little voice."

Truly chuckles. "Oh, honey, there's nothing truer than that."

And it is true, because tonight, I'm listening to another voice.

18

That voice says *Get to know her.*

Once my sister heads to the end of the bar, Sloane sets down her drink, crosses her legs, and rubs her palms together. "Tell me what you've been up to. Tell me how you've been for the last few years. I've run into you now and then, and obviously I've seen you at work for the last week, but I want to know how everything is. How is your mom?"

We catch up, and it's so much better than talking about work. Hell, maybe this is what we needed—this night to reconnect on a new level. To reconnect as colleagues, or perhaps even as friends. It's dangerous to contemplate anything else.

I tell her that my mom has retired from jingle writing and is doing what she truly loves—training dogs. Her own dogs. I ask her about Brooklyn, and she tells me about the tiny thimble of an apartment she has there, but how she makes the best of it, shoehorning in room for her laptop and sock-making accoutrements, but that's about it.

"When did you start the sock making?"

"A few years ago. It's a fun outlet for stress. Something to keep me busy."

"Sounds like you like being busy."

She smiles. "I definitely do."

"And is the sock business hopping along?" I ask playfully.

She winks. "It's my side hustle. Socks with mottos. It brings in a few extra dollars, so I can't complain. Tell me more about the clinic and how that's been."

I tell her I've loved building the vet practice, that my employees are the best, and that I admire the hell out of her father. I also admit I thought he was going to retire.

She takes a drink of champagne, seems to marinate on what I've just said, then puts down the glass. "Do you want him to?"

I go for the full truth. "Admittedly? I do. It's been my dream to run the business myself."

"Why is that?"

"Because of my dad." Sadness creeps in as I remember him, but also as I fail to recall him too. He's been dead for nearly as many years of my life as he was alive. "It was what he wanted to do. It was always his dream to own a neighborhood practice, to run it solo. He grew up here in the West Village, met my mom here, and he raised us here, so he had this whole vision of being a community vet."

"That sounds lovely."

"He wanted to be the guy who knew all the neighbors and would ask whether Tom the tuxedo was using his scratching post and if Dolly the bulldog mix was doing okay with her arthritis."

Sloane sets a hand on her heart. "I love that."

"That was one of the reasons he went into business in the first place. But when he became sick, well, he wasn't able to do it."

"Did he ask you to pick up the mantle for him?"

I swallow roughly, remembering those last days with him, the conversations, ever more brief, that we had. I shake my head. "That's the thing. He never asked me to. He never said that he wanted me to do this or that. He wanted me to pursue what I wanted in life. But I also knew that I wanted to do it for him, to complete the dream he had. Because somewhere along the way, his dream became my dream."

"You wanted the same things." She rests her cheek in her hand.

"I like knowing the people who come into the practice. I like knowing Ms. Clarke and her monkey-humping dog, Ruby, and Mr. Franklin with the blind-in-one-eye white cat. I suppose my dad's goals and mine became the same, and I wanted to own a practice here perhaps as a tribute to him. And yes, I've worked closely with Doug, and I'm a junior partner, but I'd like to be able to do it on my own. I mean that as no disrespect to your father. You know I think the world of him, and I've learned so much from the guy."

She laughs lightly. "It's okay. I didn't take it in a bad way. I don't have daddy issues, so I'm not bothered that you want him gone."

"I swear, I don't *want* him gone," I say, mostly denying the truth.

She shoots me the side-eye. "It's okay. I can tell you do."

I sigh. "It's not him. It's that I'd like to do this on my own. But how is it for you working with him? Is it weird or tense at all?" I ask, glad that we can discuss him as her father rather than as the very real obstacle in our universe.

She purses her lips, seems to noodle on this, then nods. "It's actually fine. My parents split up when I was three, and there was never a ton of animosity, even though my mom changed my last name to hers after the divorce. I saw Dad every other weekend. I visited him during the summers. He wasn't an absentee parent, but he wasn't terribly present either, so it made for a mostly uncomplicated relationship. My mom harbored no ill will against him, so I didn't have to deal with that." She takes a drink. "I see him more now than I did when I was a kid."

"And that's good? You like that?"

"We actually have a lot in common, being in the same business. So it's kind of cool to bond over animal welfare. I'm close with my mom, and was definitely close with her growing up, so maybe this is just my time to connect with him more."

And that's another reminder to resist the woman.

This is her chance to spend time with her dad in a way she wasn't able to growing up. Far be it from me to get in the way. If my dad were here, I know I'd want to spend time with him.

I raise a glass. "To family. To fathers."

She lifts her champagne. "To the ones we have, and the ones in our hearts."

My throat tightens, but I swallow past the roughness and take a drink. "Tell me more about your mom. What's she like?" I ask, thinking that will be the safer parent to talk about.

Sloane's eyes twinkle. "You'll understand everything about me when I tell you. My mom's a hippy, a laid-back animal lover who rescued every three-legged dog and tailless cat she found."

"The apple didn't fall far from the tree."

"I was definitely cut from the same cloth, and I'm sure I wound up in rescue because of her rather than because of Dad. We always rescued animals growing up. My mom would see a lost dog and move heaven and earth to return it to where it belonged. But I'm also a lot like my father. He's more intense. Always working. Always thinking."

"That's exactly like Doug."

"He's more wound up than her. More type A, and I'm the same in that way. I've never been good at getting out of my own head. I'm always thinking about the next thing I want to do. For a while when I was much younger, I thought I wanted to be an actress. I was even in a play in college."

I smile, imagining Sloane onstage. "I wouldn't have been able to take my eyes off you."

She scoffs. "Oh, you would've, because I was terrible at it. You would have cringed."

I arch a brow. "Are you sure?"

"I was the worst," she says, finishing her champagne as I empty my Scotch. We order another round, and she returns to the subject. "I was terrible. I had a heartfelt speech to deliver in an original play I was in. And I just wasn't present. I was thinking about what papers I had due the next day, or what causes I was going to work on next. I wasn't fully invested. So I chose to do something I could put all of my head and my heart into at the same time."

"And are you happy giving all of your head and heart to rescue?"

She nods vigorously. "Yes. Definitely yes. I love it. Thank you for encouraging me to do it."

"We were instrumental to each other, it seems." Truly slides us the fresh drinks, and I knock back more Scotch. "So what about you? What did you do over the last seven years? And please don't mention Plant or Brick or anyone like that."

She shoots me a flirty smile, then mimes zipping her lips. She unzips them, though, to talk. "I got a master's, and I worked in some other charities in development, and that's how I knew for sure I wanted to open my own rescue."

"And presumably you've been completely single

the entire time and have never dated anyone?" I ask, deadpan and praying.

Her expression is 100 percent serious. "Not a soul. I absolutely didn't date anyone at all."

I lift my glass. "Excellent. I will drink to that."

She smacks my arm. "And yet it's okay for you to have been a man about town?"

I arch a brow. "How do you know I was a man about town?"

She gives me a thorough once-over. "Look at you. That's really your flaw. You're too good-looking. And you're too charming. You've had women all over you, haven't you?"

"Is that a flaw? Also, do you really want me to answer that?"

Sighing, she shakes her head and takes a drink. "I don't really want to know." She takes a breath then nods. "Actually, I do. Were you involved with anyone serious? I do want to know that."

I scratch my jaw, remembering Lucy, Kelly, Lilah.

"There were a few women who I was serious about, but no one I saw myself having a long future, or a meaningful one, with." I brace myself to ask the same. "What about you?"

She shakes her head. "There were a couple of guys here and there. You meet someone, you think it's going to work out, you think you have a lot in common, and then it turns out that he wants to spend his whole weekend watching sports."

"Hey, now!"

"I'm just saying, you're flawed."

"And you've discovered my flaw evidently." I narrow my eyes. "But do you truly think I don't listen to the little voice on my shoulder?"

"I don't know. Do you ignore it? What's it been telling you tonight?"

"It's been telling me that you and I are becoming friends," I say, but my tone isn't entirely friendly.

Her lips curve up. "Is that so? We're friends?"

"Feels that way." But it actually feels like we're in Tahiti again. And tonight is its own separate night, apart from time and space and reason.

"It does feel that way," she agrees softly. "Do you think we found that alternate universe you mentioned?"

I inch closer. "I'd like to spend a night in that alternate universe."

She licks her lips. "Everything's different there."

"Nothing's off-limits there."

"Maybe that's where we are." The words come out a little husky, a lot sexy, and I know what's changing.

The reminder of who she is, how we're connected, isn't keeping me away.

The barrier isn't strong enough tonight.

No matter how much we talk.

No matter how hard we try to be friends or colleagues or business partners.

The wall can't hold.

The kind of chemistry we have doesn't disappear with the snap of your fingers or the flip of a switch.

Yes, I want this newfangled friendship. Yes, I want all our various business arrangements to go swimmingly. And tangoing with someone I work with in close quarters is all kinds of risky.

But hell, this woman and I, we have a lot of unfinished business.

And I want to finish it.

Tonight.

I set a hand on her leg, spreading my palm over the fabric covering her thigh. She trembles under my touch. "There's something I've been wondering," I say, my fingers playing with her dress.

Her voice is a feather. "What's that?"

I don't take my eyes off her. Traveling along her body, I wrap my hand around her hip, tightening my grip. The feel of her is intoxicating.

I've definitely had more than one drink. I've had a whole bottle.

And I want another.

I move my hand to her face, cupping her cheek, sliding my thumb over her lip. "I can't stop wondering if you taste like champagne."

Her eyes are etched with desire, blazing with heat. "Why don't you find out?"

19

A voice says *Do it.*

It's not a little voice. It's not Truly's voice.

It's in *my* head, and it's all mine.

And, honestly, it's probably connected straight to my libido, since *that* voice has the tendency to override everything else in moments like this.

Like, for instance, good judgment.

Like warnings from business partners too.

I dip my face to hers, savoring every sliver of a second. Her glossy pink lips part the slightest bit, an invitation.

I take my time, because I want to experience every moment of kissing her again. I dust my thumb over the corner of her lips and seal my mouth to hers, capturing her kiss.

Seven long years unfurl. The moment on the street the other week was a mere snapshot. A five-second trailer to tease the audience, to leave them wanting more. This is the opening credits. The start of the whole story, unfolding on screen.

Her lips part, welcoming me. Roping her arms around my neck, she brings herself closer as I sweep my lips over hers.

Our mouths explore. Touching. Discovering. Tasting.

My brain goes hazy, and as I deepen the kiss, I'm nothing but sensations that overwhelm all else.

It's sparklers waving, lighting up the darkened sky on a hot summer night.

It's the exhilarating first dip of a sixty-mile-per-hour roller coaster.

It's the first sip of a vintage Scotch. A taste that makes you moan. That makes your mouth water and crave so much more.

Kissing Sloane is everything good in the world. She tastes like champagne, and it goes to my head. Her hair smells like vanilla, and it floods my senses. I want to kiss her breathless. Yanking her closer, I grind against her, needing her to feel how much I want her. She groans as she clearly gets my message.

Then she sends her own message, wrapping her hands tighter around my neck. She's fierce, kissing me harder, rougher.

It's like past times and it's like present times, because there's a brand-new urgency between us.

My pulse spikes and my blood heats. It's as if a clock is ticking. Hell, time's speeding up, spinning faster.

I'm vaguely aware we're in public.

But I don't care because the woman I've wanted for years is rubbing against the outline of my cock. Her fingers dart to my hair, tugging. "Harder, more," she pants.

Damn, those are two of my favorite words.

I give her a rough, demanding kiss, but soon she breaks it, taking a moment to breathe, to smooth her hair.

"So how are we doing as friends?" she asks, a naughty glint in her lovely brown eyes.

I need a second to recalibrate, since we just went from racing around the track to a leisurely drive.

"I'd say we're great friends in our alternate universe." I lower my face and kiss her neck, whispering, "If friends do this . . ."

Adjusting the pace, I leave a trail of kisses along the column of her throat, her murmurs the soundtrack to my path up to her ear. I nibble on the shell, since she seems to need a respite from the intensity.

"Your alternate universe has funny rules." She slides a hand around the back of my head and tugs me back.

Claiming my lips.

Saying *You're mine.*

Oh, hell yeah. She can have me.

The brief respite is over.

She kisses with fire. With determination. With a hot, hungry need. She's vibrating with desire, thrumming with sexual energy. This kiss is a collision, hands sliding into hair, bodies crashing together, teeth and tongue and nothing left behind. We're storming the night, marching into town, taking no prisoners.

The clatter of glasses and the murmur of voices reminds me where we are. I snap my eyes open to find Truly behind the bar, filling a glass, shaking her head. She mouths, *Get a room.*

That voice?

That's the voice I should listen to.

I meet Sloane's gaze then go for it. Because this night has only one destination. "We should go to Tahiti."

"Tonight?"

"Too long a flight?"

She lets go of my hand and holds up her thumb and forefinger. "Maybe a little. Not that I'm turning down a trip to Tahiti. Wait? Are you saying you want to take me to Tahiti? Because I can pack like *that.*"

Smiling, I slide my hand to her ass, squeezing. I whisper roughly in her ear, "I'm saying I'd like to escape with you. Like we're getting away for the night. Let's fuck away all this hot, wild desire."

She exhales then goes quiet, perhaps lost in thought. "But I thought we were going to resist kissing."

I brush the backs of my fingers along her jaw. "We already failed that test."

She pouts. "I was supposed to be an un-vixen."

"Didn't work. You're the opposite, and I want you

so fucking much." I press against her. "You have me so wound up. I'm pretty sure you're wound up too."

She pushes back. "You know I am. You know I want you too. That was never the issue."

I have to get closer to her. I need to have her. "Let's give in. Just once." I slide my fingers into her hair, she leans her head against my palm, and I continue making my case. "I can take you places. I can make you feel extraordinary, like I've always wanted to."

She hums. "You're making it hard to say no."

"True. I'm very hard to resist."

A smile spreads across her face. "You are, Malone. You're terribly, impossibly hard to resist." She nibbles on her bottom lip. "One night. Our secret. What happens in Tahiti stays in Tahiti."

"Absolutely," I say as my dick high-fives me.

"And where is this alternate universe?"

I curl my fingers around her hip bone. "My place isn't far. There's also a hotel down the block. Either way, I intend to strip you naked, get my lips all over you, and make you feel as fucking good as you looked when you were watching me sing."

She shudders. "I looked good when I was watching you? How so?"

I run my thumb over her hip, rubbing in slow, sensual circles. "You're so seductive. You looked so incredibly alluring. You looked exactly as you are— the most beautiful woman I've ever met." My fingers stray to her belly, gliding down the fabric of her dress toward my final destination. "And you and I have unfinished business."

She leans her head back, and the most delicious moan ever recorded escapes her lips. When she raises her face, she tap-dances her fingers down my chest then runs them over the silk of my tie. "Are you saying we're going to finish the business tonight?"

"Yes, and then tomorrow . . . we can be friends again." The thought pains me, but I know this is the only way to deal with our reality.

"Exactly," she says, nodding her agreement. "We take a trip tonight. We get away to a remote island. And tomorrow we go back to the real world?" She's seriously considering this. Hell, I've already considered it six ways to Sunday in the span of ten seconds, and I say it's a brilliant plan.

"Let me take care of you tonight. Let me spend the night worshipping your body and driving you wild with pleasure."

"You say these things . . ."

I grin. "And?"

"And you make it impossible to walk away." She grabs my tie and tugs my face inches from hers. "But what do you think my voice says?"

I want her to say it. The permission must come from her, and I'm dying for it. "You tell me."

She brings her mouth to my ear and whispers, hot and sexy, "It says take me to Tahiti. Fuck me hard. Fuck me good. Fuck me senseless."

That's the only voice I'm listening to tonight.

20

Sloane Elizabeth's Voice Memo to Self

&*^%$#%^&

Holy shit.

Hot damn.

Shake it off. Shake off the nerves. You're going to be fine. This is Malone. This is the man you want. He's out there, getting a hotel room.

And OH MY GOD.

You're about to get naked.

With him.

The man you've been dying for.

The object of all your fantasies.

The main attraction, the music you and the silver dolphin trip the light fantastic to.

Did you feel what he was packing?

Of course you did, you dirty bird. You felt it, and you wanted it, and you're about to get it.

Breathe.

Breathe more.

It's going to be amazing. It's going to turn your world upside down. You're going to experience a brand-new meaning of pleasure.

Just get the hell out of here and go climb that man now.

Good thing you brought condoms. You're seriously such a planner. It's killing you.

Oh, shut up. Planning is good.

Go plan on having an orgasm or two.

21

There's just something about hotels after midnight.

Plus, that Otis dude? The guy who invented elevators? I'd like to award him the Pride of the Brotherhood medal right the fuck now.

Because hotel elevators were made for foreplay.

With the mirrors, sleek chrome, and the rattle and hum, it's like a prelude to the main attraction.

As soon as the doors whisk shut—hell, *as* they're whisking shut—I grab Sloane. I spin her around, press her up against the mirrored wall, and crush her mouth to mine. She grabs at me, her hands in my hair, her nails against my scalp. We're all heat and urgency, like we both need our fix.

Lust ricochets through my veins as I hike up her leg, hooking it around my hip, grinding against her.

She moans my name and arches her back, her curves fitting perfectly against me.

We reach our floor, panting. We spill out of the

elevator and into the hall, and I drape an arm around her shoulder, bringing her close. I can't stop touching her. My lips want to be in contact with her skin, so I kiss her cheek as we reach the room. I slide the key card against the door and push it open.

Once we're inside, she's a tiger. Pouncing at me. Pushing me against the closed door, clawing at my shirt, ripping at my tie. It's like she's afraid she's going to miss something if she slows down.

I'm not looking for a long, lingering seven-course meal, but I'd like our first time to last more than five minutes, and she's operating at a speed-demon pace.

I grab her wrists. "Hey. Let me look at you."

She draws a deep breath, almost as if she's nervous. "Okay."

I arch a brow. "Are you? Okay?"

She nods several times.

"You're not okay."

She presses her palms to my chest. "I'm great. I swear. I want this."

"Just wanted to make sure." I dip my face to her neck, pressing a soft kiss to her sweet-smelling skin. She trembles, seeming to come down a notch from predator-on-the-Serengeti level. "You taste so good." I brush my lips along her neck, up to her ear, nibbling.

She murmurs as I go, and that's better. This pace is better.

I'm all for a quick screw now and then, but not now. I've waited far too long for this moment to rush it. I intend to enjoy every single second.

My hands reach around her back, splaying across her bare skin. "By the way, you can always wear dresses like this. Just in case you were wondering."

"Glad to know it has your fashion seal of approval."

"But I'm also damn curious how it looks . . . off."

She nibbles on her lip. "Take it off, Malone."

I slide the straps down, and she lets them fall to her waist. Just like that, she's revealed, and my mouth goes dry. Her breasts are beautiful teardrops, with dusky rose nipples. I would like to spend the night with my face buried between them.

I cup them both, and she stretches against me, murmuring, sighing.

Running my thumbs over her nipples, I feel them harden as I explore her. Her breath comes faster, staggered.

"*Ohhhhh.*"

That. Sound.

It's a straight shot of lust. It turns my dick to granite, and it was already imitating rock. "You're spectacular. Do you have any idea how hard it's been the last week? How much I've wanted you?"

There's something freeing about telling the woman you want how deeply you crave her. That's never been the holdup, and because it's not, I'm going to embrace the chance to tell her.

She shoots out a hand, grabs my tie. "I'm betting it's as much as I want you."

I groan, loving her need, craving her want. I slide

her dress over her hips as she kicks off her heels. She's down to nothing but a lacy black G-string, and she's everything I've dreamed she'd be.

She's strong and toned, but with a softness to her curves too, a femininity that's siren-like. Her smooth, pale skin is like a beacon to me, and she smells divine. That vanilla smell is her scent, her signature, and it drives me wild.

"As much as I'd love to have up-against-the-wall sex, right now I want you spread out on a bed, woman," I say, then in one quick move, I hoist her up over my shoulder.

She squeals, pounding her fists playfully against my back. "Malone!"

"Watch out, or I'll tickle you." I carry her to the bed as she laughs.

I set her down on the mattress and drink in the luscious sight. "Damn. You nearly naked on a hotel bed. Is this heaven?"

She rests on her elbows, watching me stare at her. "You like what you see?"

I lean over her, run a hand up her bare leg. "I love what I see. Did you think I wouldn't?"

She shakes her head. "No. I just want you to."

There are those nerves again. I don't want her to feel an ounce of them.

I wrap a hand around the back of her head and haul her in for a kiss. "I want you. I want you all to myself. I want you all night."

A small smile seems to tug at her lips. She likes my

answer. "Malone." She says my name like it's a cherry rolling around on her tongue. "I'd really like you to get naked."

Well.

The woman has spoken. The jacket comes off, and we're a well-oiled machine, making quick work of my clothes until I'm down to my boxers, and her eyes go wide.

They bug out.

"Nice dick," she says in a reverent whisper.

Mine stands up taller. Well, dicks do like to be admired.

I shed my boxer briefs, give my hard cock a stroke, and then crawl over her. "Now, what are we going to do about this lovely little piece of lace?" I slide my hand between her legs, cupping her, feeling the slick outline of her wet panties. "Hmm. Let's see if I can get it off you."

I kiss my way down her belly, and she arches against my mouth, looping her hands in my hair as I go. "God, you smell amazing."

Her hips shoot up, and my God, this woman is a live wire. One kiss and she's moaning. One touch and she's writhing.

I kiss the top of her panties, then slide them off. My entire body crackles with obscene appreciation. Her pussy is beautiful. Perfect, pink, glistening.

I lick my lips and thank my lucky stars. Then I flinch in surprise as she points at the door. "You're kicking me out?"

"No. Please. I'm not stupid. I dropped my purse when we walked in. There's a condom in it."

"I have one too, but I like that you brought one."

She winks. "More than one."

I head for the entryway, grab her purse, and bring it to her. Dipping her hand in, she finds the protection and thrusts a condom at me.

"Fine, fine. You want me just for my dick. I get it."

"Do you blame me? It's a very nice dick."

"Nice? It's nice?"

She sits up taller, wraps her hand around my cock, and squeezes. I shudder as a wave of pleasure rolls over me. The feel of her hand is tremendous. As she runs her palm up and down, I let my eyes float closed, savoring the pure heat of this moment. The fire that crackles in my veins. The desire that floods my body. The woman I lust after to inordinate degrees is touching my most favorite body part, and I'm about to fuck her.

I must have been very good in a past life.

And in *this* life, I need to get inside her and drive her wild.

I open the condom wrapper and roll it on. She watches me the whole time, her brown eyes blazing. After I pinch the top, I settle between her legs and rub the head of my cock against her slickness.

Her mouth parts in a delicious O, and she moans.

I push inside, and the second I feel her warmth hugging my cock, the pleasure shoots to another level.

Sparks rain over my skin, and I feel electric, white-hot as I fill her.

She wraps her legs around my back, hooking her ankles together.

"This is worth waiting for," I murmur, as I begin to move. "You're worth waiting for."

"So worth it," she pants.

Swiveling my hips, I search for the ideal rhythm for her. She loops her hands tighter around my neck, bringing my mouth close to hers.

That works for me. That works just fine, and I lower my chest closer, bracing myself on my palms as I thrust. We set a pace, and it's fantastic. We're in sync, rocking and grinding, moaning and groaning. Hands squeezing, fingers tightening.

"What do you like best, sweetheart? What gets you there?" I ask.

She shakes her head. *"This."* It's all she says. Just *"This,"* as she closes her eyes and sighs, a sexy, lingering sound that sends shivers down my spine.

I follow her lead, fucking her just like *this*, each thrust punctuated by her moans, and soon she's rocking faster up against me, her voice growing louder.

"Can you . . .?"

"You want me to touch your sweet clit while I do this?" I supply, taking an educated guess.

She smiles. "Yes."

"Let's get you on top, then. How does that sound?"

She shakes her head. "Can you fuck me from behind?"

I scoff. "Can I? Can I fuck you from behind? I'd like nothing better."

We maneuver our way to a new position, one that's carnal and dirty as she gets on all fours, lowering her back. With my palm spread over her ass, I slide back inside.

"I feel it," she whispers. "So much deeper."

"So much," I echo as my bones shake, rattling with lust and need. I pump into her, enjoying the view of her hair spilling down her back, her ass in the air.

I run a hand along her back. "Now this is a gorgeous view."

"You came to Tahiti and took in the sights." She sighs contentedly as she pushes back against me.

Bringing both hands to her hips, I yank her closer, driving deeper, then I band my arm around her waist, gliding my thumb between her legs.

She cries out when I first touch her clit, and that's my cue to keep going. I rub the delicious rise of her as she rocks on my dick, thrusting onto my cock as much as she can.

I keep up the pace that she likes—fast, hard, but never forgetting about that glorious nub between her legs, making sure she's loving everything as I stroke circles on her clit.

With each stroke, she moans.

With each thrust, she cries out.

And then she cries louder. "I'm close, so close."

My job is simple—*don't fuck up*.

I'm a master of self-control, so I stave off my own orgasm, gritting my teeth and focusing on hers, damn near willing it. I rub and stroke and fuck, and all I can think is her orgasm is going to be epic.

Because her moans are. Her cries are. Her sounds are the stuff of legend. Her noises are unlocking my pleasure, and her own seems to be hurtling through her. "Oh God, I'm coming."

Her cry starts loud, then shoots even louder. She's all *ohhh God* and *yes, yes, yes*, and it's fantastic how vocal she is.

Really, it is.

Except my suspicions are confirmed when she lets out a long, over-the-top, glorious sigh as she slumps down under me, like she's sated and blissed out.

She just faked an orgasm.

That's a first.

At least, I think so.

For a hot second, I travel through time. As I head to the restroom to toss the condom, I revisit ghosts of my sex life past.

Kelly from college, with the trumpet-like orgasmic cries.

Lilah, who lived in Chelsea and writhed like she was a belly dancer when she came.

Sonya, whose O face was the poster child for O faces.

They were all epic comers.

Weren't they?

Wait.

Have I been Sally'd in the diner by them all? Have all men everywhere been Sally'd every time?

But as I stare at my reflection, I shake my head. *Nah.* Because here's the thing with Sloane.

I knew instantly.

I wasn't fooled.

Sloane faked it, but she didn't fake me out.

She went too far. She overacted, oversold her climax, and I wasn't buying it. That's not something anyone else I've been with has ever done.

I shove away thoughts of exes and focus solely on Sloane's non–Academy Award performance.

But why did she try to pull off the act?

She didn't like it?

No way.

Maybe I am too cocky, but I don't buy that. We were both into it, every step of the way. From the bar, to the elevator, to the room, to the bed.

When we switched positions too.

And besides, I felt *her*, I touched *her*. She *was* into it. She's one of the most responsive women I've ever encountered.

Yet, she didn't fly over the edge, and she definitely wanted to.

I turn on the tap, splash some water on my face, and turn it off. I grab a towel and dry off. I have a plan.

This is a problem, and I'm going to treat it like I would a poodle who's not "acting like himself."

I can't exactly ask the patient what's wrong. But I can deduce this—since Sloane deliberately faked it, she must have a reason.

I need to get to the bottom of that.

And I know how to do it.

I'll take a lesson from her playbook.

I'll fake it too.

I'll pretend I believe she came like a world-class orgasm-er.

I return to the bed, ready to conduct my recon.

She's stretched out on her side, her head propped in her hand, her blonde hair spilling over her fingers and falling down on the bed. "Hey," she says, her voice a little sleepy-sexy. Is that a ruse too, the post-sex gravel in her tone?

"Hey, beautiful." I lie next to her, and the second I touch the mattress, her hands are on me, traveling up my chest and down over my hip.

She's a frisky one.

I note that in my mental spy journal.

Spy Log Detail One: eager beaver.

"That was . . ." she begins, trailing off, and I'm half-tempted to fill in the sentence with snark. *That was quite a performance! Will there be another show tonight?* But that approach won't glean any intel. Going along with it will.

"Amazing," I supply.

Her hand spreads across my chest. "Yes, totally amazing."

"Like you'd hoped it would be?" I arch a questioning brow.

She smiles, a dopey, happy grin. "Yes, Exactly."

Spy Log Detail Two: she definitely wants me to believe that O was real.

I loop my arm around her, tugging her close.

"Damn, woman. I have dreamed about you for years. To finally have you was incredible." I press my lips to her cheek, her eyelid, her nose. Then I kiss her mouth, in a soft, lingering way that promises deeper kisses to come.

"It was, Malone. It was totally incredible." She adopts a cheeky expression, raising her eyebrows and dancing her fingers across my chest. "Can we go to Tahiti again tonight?"

Spy Log Detail Three: She wants to screw again. That makes me think she liked the sex. Or at least liked it enough.

I scoff. "We're still here. We need to take full advantage of all the amenities."

Her fingers travel down my stomach. "So . . . how long do we stay here? All night?"

I look at her and tuck a finger under her chin, fishing for more clues. "Is that what you want?"

She rolls her eyes. "No, I want you to kick me out."

I gesture to the door. "See you later, woman. I'm going to enjoy this king-size bed all by myself."

She swats my elbow, climbs on top of me, and grabs my wrists. "Take that back."

Spy Log Detail Four: The woman is playful AF. She's got to be into me.

I slide my arms above my head so she falls onto me, her breasts temptingly near my face. I raise my neck, suck on one delicious nipple.

She lets out a sexy sigh.

Spy Log Detail Five: she seems turned on again.

She starts rocking against me as I lavish attention on her. When she pulls away, she slides down my body, straddling my growing length, rubbing against it, letting me know she's still wet.

Spy Log Detail Six: She wants to screw so she can get the O she missed. Grab a condom and finish the job, dick.

Spy Log Detail Seven: Idiot. You still don't know why she faked it. Cool your jets.

I resume my routine, untangling myself from her hands and flipping her to her back. "You want to spend the night here? Get this out of our system so we can go back to work on Monday like nothing happened?"

A frown crosses her face, but then she nods dutifully.

I tilt my head. "You don't like that idea?"

Her eyes turn sad. "I know it's what we need to do, but I like being with you, Malone."

My heart thumps hard. It hammers. She sounds so real. So vulnerable.

I drop my mask and run my fingers across her cheek. "Yeah, me too. Which makes me curious . . ."

She knits her brow. "About what?"

I dot a kiss to her lips. No animosity. No accusation. Just an inquiry. "Why you faked it."

Her jaw drops.

23

Sloane Elizabeth's Mental Voice Memo to Self

Busted.

Think fast.

Lightning fast.

What to do?

Do you improvise? Deny? Cover it up?

You could fashion a fabulous story. Say, "What, are you crazy? Of course I came, and it was awesome."

Because it was. That was the best sex ever. The best almost-O ever. The best everything ever. That's no lie. Everything about tonight was worthy.

But there's this thing that hangs over you. That haunts you.

The Thing.

And The Thing has bedeviled you since forever.

Time to own up?

Girl, it's been since the twelfth of never that you've had an orgasm through sex. Might as well confess.

The jig is up.

24

It's like watching a time-lapse video of someone's day.

Her expression shifts through fifty variations.

The telltale *oops* to *What, are you crazy?* to something I'll bet goes like this—*Better just get this off my chest.*

Because it seems that's where she's headed when she sighs heavily.

"Because I can't come through intercourse," she blurts out. "I'm sorry."

Whoa. I was *not* expecting sledgehammer bluntness. "You can't? You never have?" I'm flooded with curiosity. The morbid kind. Because that sounds like a living hell. This woman. The suffering. My God.

She shakes her head. "Never."

I sputter, "Not once?"

"That would be the definition of 'never.' Never, as in not once."

My eyes bug out. I can't believe this tale of woe. "You've literally never had an orgasm through sex?"

She frowns as she nods. "Literally. It's not like I'm happy about it."

"But . . ." I'm stumped, flummoxed, shocked.

She laughs softly, a self-deprecating sound. "And look, this is most definitely a case of 'it's not you, it's me.'" She runs her hand down my arm. "I'm sorry."

"Yeah. I'm sorry, too, that you've never experienced the greatest thing ever. I should send you a bouquet. Some chocolates. Get VIP tickets to a concert to make up for the horror you're enduring."

She shakes her head and squeezes my biceps. "No, Malone. I'm sorry I faked it with you. That's what I'm apologizing for. That wasn't cool."

I scoff. There are much bigger things that concern me. Like orgasms. Or the lack thereof. "No. What's not cool is you not coming. That's what's not cool."

She offers a conciliatory smile. "Well, yeah. But I should have been honest with you. Seriously. And I'm truly sorry I did it."

My brow knits, curiosity gnawing at me. If she's never tripped into O Town through sex, why did she feel the need to go full Meg Ryan with me? "Why did you fake it, then?"

She sighs like a sad trombone. "Because I like you."
Ohhhhhh.

"Yeah?" This makes me ridiculously happy, but also perplexed. "But I still don't understand why you went for the Oscar." I run my fingers over the ends of her hair. "By the way, you suck at faking an orgasm."

"No one else has noticed."

I roll my eyes. "I'm not like those other guys."

Except I am. I have a lot in common with them evidently. And I don't want a jacket to this club.

"I know. You're not. The sex was fantastic. That's why I faked it."

I hold up a hand. "How could the sex be fantastic? You didn't come. Ergo, it couldn't have been great. News flash: *coming helps make it great.*"

"For the record, sex can be amazing for a woman even without an orgasm."

I flub my lips. "That's not possible. That's like when the losing team in the Super Bowl says it was an honor just to be there."

She shakes her head, sitting up straighter. "So sex is just a game? It's about winning or losing?"

"No, it's not. I'm not saying that whatsoever. But seriously, Sloane. All things being equal, would you rather have the big O or no O?"

"Obviously, I'd rather my body threw a freaking parade, with trumpets, a band, and the whole nine yards. But sex isn't about just the orgasm." Her tone is passionate, as if she's making a speech.

"Why isn't it?" I toss back, playing devil's advocate, because I don't buy her theory that orgasms are an afterthought. Orgasms are *the* motherfucking thought.

She nudges me with her elbow. "Oh, c'mon. An

orgasm lasts for thirty seconds. Good sex should last longer. If the whole part before the orgasm is no good, what's the point of the O?"

I shake my head. "That's like saying looking at a mouthwatering piece of cherry pie is just as good as eating it. You don't simply want to look at the pie. You want to devour the pie too." I take a beat then slide my hand down her belly. "For the record, I also want to devour you, so you're both the pie and the observer of the pie in that metaphor."

She holds up a finger to make a point. "But you can enjoy the high from the smell, maybe even take a bite of the pie. Not everyone eats an entire slice."

I give her a most skeptical look. "But is one little nibble of a delicious cherry pie enough?"

She runs her hand through my hair. "It was enough for me. It was great. You need to understand that. I felt it everywhere. Tingles spread through my body. It was intense; it was electric." Her tone dips lower, a little smoky, a lot sexy. She shivers as she describes how she felt, almost as if she's feeling it again. "I want you to know that."

"Thank you," I say, taking the compliment like a gentleman, since that seems to be important to her. "But I still want you to feel as good as you possibly can. I want you to experience *la petite mort.*"

"Me too. And I wanted to. And I thought I might. I was hoping I might. I felt like I was racing to the edge. For a few minutes, I was sure it was going to happen. I had it clutched in the palm of my hand. But then it's like it disappeared, and I knew I wasn't going to."

"Why do you think you don't come?"

She taps her temple. "I'm in my head too much."

I nod, marinating on this information, then diving deeper. "Where was your head fifteen minutes ago when you knew you weren't going to come?"

"I was thinking about how it was our first time together. How much I wanted it. How great it would be to finally come, and once I thought that, my orgasm ran away."

Everything clicks into place. "You think too much. You don't relax."

"Ya suppose?"

I laugh at her droll reply. "And you think too hard about coming. You put pressure on yourself."

She shrugs as if conceding the point. "Perhaps."

The doctor in me continues to probe the problem, hunting for a solution. "Can you come in other ways?"

She nods. "Vibrator mostly."

I flick out my tongue, asking the question.

"Sometimes."

I waggle my fingers.

"Now and then."

"But the vibrator always works?"

"Complete success. Never fails."

I shake my head in frustration. "*Vibrators.* I swear. They're going to replace men soon. You won't need us."

"We kind of don't for the most part."

"Thanks," I say drily. "But back to the case. You *can* come. There's nothing impeding you physically. No underlying condition. So basically you are a total type A in bed. Which explains why you attacked me like a tiger."

Her jaw drops. She's incredulous. "What are you talking about?"

"You were going quickly so you wouldn't have to contemplate a thing. But here's what I think."

She shoots me an amused grin. "Do tell, *pussy* doctor."

A laugh bursts from me. "I am indeed the pussy doc, and here's my prognosis for your gorgeous, sexy, glorious pussy. You're stuck in a rut. You haven't come, so you think you can't, so you try to not think, and that's like saying *Don't picture cats while I talk to you about cats.* And all you think about are cats."

She gives me a quizzical look. "Would you like me to think about kitties while you fuck me?"

"Yes and no." I pretend to put on a stethoscope and act as if I'm examining her. She laughs as I move the imaginary stethoscope over her throat. "Yup. You've lost your purr."

She imitates a feline who's pleased.

"Not buying it. That was fake. But don't worry. We're going to get your purr back."

"Get it back? Doctor, I've never had it."

"That's the saddest story I've ever heard, but I'm an optimist." I run my finger down her side by her breast, along the curve of her waist as goose bumps rise on her skin. "And a scientist and a problem-solver. Also, I'm willing to sacrifice myself to the cause."

"What cause is that?"

"Your orgasm cause. That's the only cause that matters. We're going to crack the case."

She lifts a skeptical brow. "We?"

I nod, resolute. "Yes. We."

"In one night?"

I wave a hand dismissively. "Please. That's not enough time. I need a week. We're going to spend a week in Tahiti, and I promise by the end of the seven days, I'll get you purring. It's a one hundred percent satisfaction guaranteed promise."

She laughs, then it fades, replaced by a tinge of resignation. "Malone, I love the idea, but there are a million reasons we can't do that."

But I'm a persistent bastard. Especially when something as life-sustaining as a climax is at stake. "To come or not to come. That is the question. Whether 'tis nobler in the mind to suffer the slings and arrows of outrageous faking. Or to take arms against a sea of non-climaxes and by opposing end them."

Her laughter bubbles up again. "Okay, so you're trying to convince me by Hamleting me."

"Because this is a very Shakespearean tale. You not coming is a tragedy." I grab her hand, clasp it. "But we can rewrite it."

"How? Isn't it going to be difficult?"

"Well, not as difficult as unearthing the Sinatra

bootleg album of him singing at the Avalon Ballroom. Easier than locating a three-hundred-year-old ship-wreck off the coast of the Florida Keys."

She rolls her eyes. "I'm glad you think finding my lost O is easier than tracking down the buried trea-sure of Frank Sinatra."

"I've been hunting that one for years. But all the guys who make trades are shady, so I haven't found it yet." I run my hand down her stomach. "But your climax? That I can absolutely do. Give me a week, and I'll have you curling your toes, clutching the sheets, and arching your back." I take a beat, giving her my best sultry stare. "You'll be purring, Sloane."

Her eyes twinkle like she enjoys that prospect. "I do want to purr. I definitely do." She sighs. "But what about the one-night-only thing?"

I slam a fist on the bed. Time for another impas-sioned speech. "None of that matters. This is a triage mission, woman. Don't you get it? I have a higher call-ing. Making you come is literally all that matters."

"How are you going to get my purr back?"

"Lessons. I'm going to give you lots of lessons. I will be your butler delivering you Os on demand. Your concierge at the five-star hotel of the meaning of life. Because that's what orgasms are."

She slides closer to me. "You're saying we're staying in Tahiti at Malone's Luxury Resort of Earth-Shattering, Spine-Tingling, Toe-Curling Os?"

"It'll be the best trip you ever take."

I slide my way down her body, kissing her belly as

I go. When I reach the top of her mound, she's wriggling against me. "Are you starting tonight?" she whispers, a hopeful look in her brown eyes.

I laugh and move back up to her face, dropping a kiss to her lovely lips. "No way."

She pouts. "Why not?"

"Sweetheart, for a project this important, a man does not start without reinforcements. We will begin on Monday."

"Then, for the first time ever, I'm really looking forward to a Monday."

25

Sloane Elizabeth's Post-It Note for Sunday's Important Tasks

1. Go underwear shopping.

2. See #1.

3. Also, consider massage, yoga, meditation, and any other techniques for shutting off that annoying brain that's getting in the way.

4. Ooh! Idea! Tickle the pink ivories before you see him. No pressure then, right?

5. Make time for #4.

6. Text Piper and tell her everything.

* * *

Sloane: So that's everything.

Piper: And that's interesting. Can we call it Project No More Thing?

Sloane: How about we refer to it as Eradicate the Orgasm Thief?

Piper: That does have a nice ring to it. Or maybe just Reversing the Thing?

Sloane: The Thing Reversal?

Piper: Love it. It feels like something that happens in a superhero movie when he has to turn back time to change the fate of the world.

Sloane: Yes, the future of humanity and climaxes have a lot in common.

Piper: Both are noble causes. However, I have one piece of advice . . .

Sloane: Of course. ;)

Piper: I'm an advice giver. It's what I do!

Sloane: It's what you do so well!

Piper: Here goes: have an open mind.

Sloane: Trust me—the mind isn't closed. The mind may even be too open. Too much is going through it at that critical moment.

Piper: What I mean is this—if this man is really committed to giving you pleasure, see what you can do to get there too.

Sloane: Like herbs, mantras, chants, voodoo, offerings, séances, and Ouija boards?

Piper: That, and maybe also just letting go of some of the past.

Sloane: Past what? What past am I clinging to?

Piper: Past boyfriends, sweetie. Let's be honest. You've dated kind of selfish pricks.

Sloane: Whoa. Tell me what you really think.

Piper: I'm just being blunt.

Sloane: AS YOU DO.

Piper: Why, thank you. *curtsies* Look, you know I've never been fond of your exes. You tend to go for guys who are a little distant, a little removed.

Sloane: That is true. I can't argue with you there.

Piper: And hey, we all have issues. I have my fair share of issues. Big thorny issues.

Sloane: True, your issues are bigger than my issues. *sticks out tongue*

Piper: You know it! Mine are a mile high. But at least I've been to the mile-high club. :)

Sloane: Show off.

Piper: Anyway, all I'm saying is have an open mind to what you want in your body, your mind, and your heart. Also, it may not have felt entirely right being intimate with the dickhead jerks you dated.

Sloane: And do you think I feel better being intimate with Malone?

Piper: I don't think it's any surprise he's the one you're playing "Midnight Train to O-ville" with.

Sloane: Perhaps he'll be the one to get me to that destination.

Piper: You know where orgasms lead.

Sloane: To bliss?

Piper: That, but also intimacy. Watch out.

Sloane: I'll consider myself warned. On that note, want to meet me at that sexy lingerie shop on the Upper East Side?

Piper: I thought you'd never ask.

26

Whoever said Sunday was a day of rest clearly never had a mission like mine.

There is no rest when you're tasked with something so critical. The pleasure of a woman is at stake, for fuck's sake.

I can't watch sports. I can't shoot hoops with Nick or Jason. I can barely even think about the jujitsu class on the schedule this evening.

I have research to do, and that's all I should be doing.

Studying and gathering data.

If I head into tomorrow night cock blazing, ego blasting, thinking I can send her soaring with my big dick, then I might as well slap an F on Project Good Loving right now.

She doesn't need a big dick—though I come equipped, thank you very much.

She doesn't need machismo either.

What she needs, I suspect, is something else entirely.

I spend the afternoon in the modern-day equivalent of the research stacks—my iPad. I rappel into the woman's cave for the day. Don't try to find me. I'm in *Cosmo*. I'm deep diving to *Refinery29*. I'm hanging out in *Bustle*.

Hell, I even search for something I never thought I'd search for before: *feminist porn*. And there is some seriously hot fucking going on thanks to that search term. The best part? Everything is all about *her*.

Her needs. Her pleasure. Her path to O.

I watch. I take notes.

I study the hell out of what a woman who's never visited the land of Oh God, There, Right There needs to reach that destination.

When I close the tablet and head to jujitsu that night, I somehow focus all my mental energy on how to make Sloane Elizabeth feel like a queen in bed, barely saying a word to Jason or Truly till we're done.

When class is over, Jason claps me on the back. "Want to grab a bite?"

I shake my head. "Nope. I have work to do."

"Sunday night veterinarian work?"

"Work of another kind," I answer. "Go hang out with Truly if you want company."

My sister stares daggers at me. "Thanks for making me a consolation prize."

Jason winks at her. "Don't be sad, Truly. You're a lovely consolation."

"Gee, thanks."

I'm off, leaving Truly and Jason staring after me as I speed-walk out of there like I've just received marching orders.

Which sounds about right.

* * *

The next day at the clinic, I am all business. I treat my patients like the pro that I am. I address staff issues like a boss. I consult with Doug like it's my job, because it is.

I am firing on eighty-eight cylinders today. The prospect of seeing Sloane tonight is an injection of pure adrenaline, pushing me through the hours.

Seeing her throughout the day also contributes to the get-shit-done-like-a-badass attitude, since my motivation is right in front of me.

Around midday, a client brings in the friendliest cat I've ever treated, who's ornery as a bull today. He has a hell of a reason for being pissed. He can't piss. I set to work on the black cat named Quinn right away, getting a catheter going for the blockage. A little later, I find Sloane visiting the feline, cooing at him through the metal bars of his kennel. "You're going to feel better real soon. I promise. Dr. Goodman is the pussycat whisperer," she says softly.

"Why, thank you."

She startles then smiles, perhaps a little embarrassed. "I didn't think anyone was back here."

"I figured as much. Also, that was adorable."

"And true, I suspect. On all counts."

"Thanks for visiting Quinn. He likes company."

She reaches in and scratches his chin, and he rubs against her. "I'm always happy to make the rounds." She tilts her head. "By the way, I wanted to ask you about a dog."

She tells me about a min-pin with a skin condition that she wants to bring into her rescue, showing me a picture of the pup as we leave the kennel section. "That was taken by the shelter I want to spring him from. But I want to make sure I'm not biting off more than I can chew. Can you help him without it becoming too onerous?"

I study the picture, nodding. "This looks highly treatable. We should have him feeling better in a few days."

She shoots me a most professional smile, and I want to kiss it right off her. Because I know what it means. It's a *we have a secret* smile. It's the *I'm working hard not to let on* look.

And it gets me going.

Knowing what we have cooking tonight is a big turn-on.

Then again, everything about her is a recipe for instant arousal, including the vanilla scent of her hair. I get a heady whiff as I stand close, so damn close to her.

"See! I knew you two would get on like a couple of old pals."

At the sound of Doug's voice, I blink and tear myself away from Sloane, even though we weren't touching. My skin prickles with an unpleasant sensation that feels distinctly like guilt and leaves an aftertaste like betrayal.

"Yes, we get along fine," Sloane says, cool and professional.

"I had a feeling." He sounds so damn proud. Doug motions for us to join him in his office. "Come. I have something for you two."

With my stomach churning and my feet leaden, I follow him. Once inside his office, he gestures to a white box on the desk, a slim blue ribbon tied around it. "For you two. And you can share them with Jonathan and Sam too."

I gesture to the box, barely able to meet Sloane's eyes. If I do, all I will see is how much I want her, and I can't deal with that right now. "You do the honors."

She clears her throat, reaches for the box, and tugs at the string. "Thanks, Dad." But her fingers are unsteady, and they slip.

I grab the box and untie it, flipping open the white cardboard flap. Inside are several dog bones with iced frosting on them.

"They're cookies. Shaped like dog bones," Doug blurts out, as if he's been bursting to reveal his surprise. "Helena made them. Try one. It's chocolate chip."

I reach for a cookie and bite. It's remarkably tasty. "It's good, Doug."

"Try one, Sloane."

She takes a cookie and chews. "Yum."

We glance at each other, and the secret between us is so thick you could turn it into a stew.

"It's just a small little gift. To say thank you," Doug adds.

My brow creases. "For what?"

Doug strides over, clapping one hand on my shoulder, one on his daughter's. "For making change look easy. Admittedly, I was nervous. How this arrangement might go. But it's been great." He looks from his daughter to me, and my guilt doubles, then doubles again, multiplying into a towering pile of coins of guilt.

I'm sleeping with his daughter.

I'm screwing her behind his back.

And I'm going to do it tonight.

And I'm going to fucking love it.

"It's been great. Working together has been great," I say roughly.

Sloane steps forward and kisses his cheek. "It's been fantastic," she adds. "And tell Helena she's one heck of a baker."

"She's a baker, she's a painter, she's a listener. I love her madly. Hey. I wanted to take her someplace for a vacation soon. Do you have any thoughts on where we should go?" His earnestness with her reminds me that she's family. She knows his wife well enough to answer the question.

And I'm a third wheel.

I turn around. "Thanks for the dog bone cookies," I say, and I don't look back. I head straight to my office, shut the door, and slump into my chair. I drop my head to my desk, groaning in frustration.

My next appointment is in ten minutes, and I need to shake off this feeling. Sitting up, I shovel my hands through my hair like I can erase the whole encounter, everything from Doug's congratulations on our *bonding* to his need to impress his wife.

I swivel around, grab a picture frame from next to my computer, and study the photo from years ago. Mom, Dad, Truly, and me at our high school graduation, a month before Dad died.

"What would you do?" I ask the man I respect, the man I admire.

But as soon as the question finds air and breath, I take it back, shaking my head, waving it away like smoke.

"Pretend I didn't say that," I mutter.

I don't want his advice.

I don't want anyone's.

I want what I want.

I don my Super Vet jacket, head to the exam room, and do my job the rest of the day.

Tonight, I have another job, and it's one I can't wait to fulfill.

I want it so much I shove everything else aside.

Out of sight, out of mind.

27

I send her a text early in the evening.

Malone: Is Vietnamese still your favorite cuisine? Or would you prefer Thai or Italian?

Sloane: I love Italian. I'm a complete sucker for pasta. I'll pretty much do anything for noodles.

Malone: Just as a reminder—you don't need to do anything. I'll be doing all the work. And the ordering. And the everything.

Sloane: I thought you were going to cook.

Malone: Considering I'm all about playing to one's strengths, I'm going to show off some of my other skills.

Sloane: And those are?

Malone: My ability to order from the finest restaurants in this city. Arrive hungry.

Sloane: Obviously. I thought we made that crystal clear. I'm incredibly hungry. Starving, you might say. For something in particular.

Sloane: By the way, what can I bring? Wine? Dessert? Batteries? The silver dolphin? A feather tickler? Rope? Crisco?

Malone: Crisco. Lots of Crisco.

Sloane: Stopping by Costco now.

Malone: And to answer your question, you can bring anything you want that makes you feel good. That's the thing, Sloane—this isn't about me telling you what to do or showing you how your body works. This is about you feeling incredible, and whatever you need to feel that way is what you should get.

Sloane: You say things like that and . . .

Malone: And what?

Sloane: And it makes me swoon.

Malone: Then I'm doing it right. But maybe save the swooning for when you get here, because then I can catch you.

Sloane Elizabeth's Post-It Note for VITAL Tasks

1. Call Basil for help. If anyone can find it, it'll be him. *Check.*

2. Don't stare at the phone all day waiting for him to call back. Have some patience. *Check.*

3. Do a victory dance when he tells you he found it! *Check.*

4. Meet Basil before going to Malone's. *Check.*

5. Grab a pretty red bow, because red bows make everything better. *Check.*

I am in music heaven.

Frank Sinatra warbles from the laptop, his fantastic voice filling the apartment. I tap a beat on the counter as we listen to his concert at the Avalon.

You couldn't wipe the grin off my face if you tried. I shake my head in admiration once more. "I can't believe you found this. In a day. I've been looking for years."

Sloane shakes her hips. "When you got it, you got it."

"You're clearly the most amazing person who ever lived. And I owe Basil a huge thank you. Now that he found Sinatra, he's no longer Plant."

"I told you you'd like him. He's a total music hound. I called him this morning and asked him to track it down for you. He found it in five hours, and it didn't cost an arm and a leg."

"A finger though?"

"I sacrificed a pinky for it. Worth it, though, for your reaction."

I loop an arm around her waist and drop a kiss onto her lips as the Chairman of the Board sings "I've Got You Under My Skin." "Fitting tune. Also, you didn't have to."

She smiles, and it's radiant. She's so damn pleased with herself for making me happy. And hell, she should be. I've been hunting for the CD for ages. "No, I didn't have to. I wanted to," she says.

Then she kisses me, and I close my eyes, letting the world fade away as the music and the woman become all there is.

When the song ends, my mission begins.

The sound she makes as she takes the first bite of pasta primavera is carnal.

She rolls her eyes and moans around the fork.

Lucky fork.

"This is incredible," she declares when she finishes the bite of olive oil–drizzled artichoke. "You do know how to order."

"World class skills at restaurant picking. I got 'em," I say then take a bite of my chicken dish. We're at the marble counter in my kitchen, parked on leather stools.

She dives in for another bite, humming as she chews. Her dark-red top slopes down her shoulder.

My attention snaps to a lacy pink strap. I file it away, though, knowing I'll be spending time removing her clothes soon enough.

After another bite, she sets down the fork and stares at me expectantly. "So what's the story with the pasta?"

"It has special silver dust in it that's known to induce spontaneous orgasms."

"In that case, I'll have multiples." She laughs as she takes another forkful. "Seriously though. This pasta is to die for."

"I'm glad you're enjoying it."

She smirks. "And will I be burning it off?"

I reach for a glass of wine, meeting her gaze. "I guess we'll have to find out."

She takes a sip of the Pinot Grigio, then licks her lips. "Tastes like peaches."

I kiss the corner of her lips, murmuring, "Good thing I like the taste of peaches."

She downs her drink, her eyes twinkling as she whispers, "Me too."

We finish, and she stares at me quizzically, gesturing to the meal. "The dinner. Is it really aphrodisiac food? I guess I think of oysters and chocolate-covered strawberries when it comes to aphrodisiacs."

I take the plates and carry them to the sink, then grab our glasses and head to the couch, motioning for her to join me on a slate-gray cushion.

She moves in next to me, and I hand her the wine. "Want to know?"

"I do. I really do."

"It's not supposed to be an aphrodisiac meal. I'm not trying to make you come with pasta."

She snaps her fingers, aw-shucks style. "But that would be quite a feat."

"If pasta is the key to coming, you can find me at Olive Garden for the rest of my days." I take a drink of the wine. "You want to know why I picked this food?"

"Because it's my favorite?"

I nod. "Brains and beauty. Yes, it's really that simple."

"But you know I'm a sure thing tonight. You don't need to buy me a fancy meal to get in my pants," she whispers conspiratorially.

"I don't?" I feign surprise.

Laughing, she indulges in a sip then sets down the wine. "Seriously though. The meal was amazing. Thank you."

"Good. The last thing I want on your mind in the heat of the moment is how long till you can grab a slice of pizza or a ham sandwich." I shudder. "I mean, I'm good. But I don't want to have to compete with a ham sandwich."

"Or with New York's best cheese pie, for that matter. Let's be honest—if I have to choose between Famous Ray's and sex, that's a tough call."

I scoff. "Please. Choose the pizza. Every time." I set down my wineglass and take a moment to enjoy the view. Blonde hair, swept up. Skinny jeans. A top that keeps giving me the most tantalizing peek at her lingerie.

And those lips.

Dear God, those bee-stung lips.

She licks them, looking a little nervous. "Hi," she whispers.

"Hi."

"Thanks for inviting me over tonight."

"Thanks for coming."

She smiles. "I thought about it most of the day. Even when . . . maybe even especially when . . ."

She doesn't need to fill in the blanks. I know exactly what she means. "Was that weird for you? When your dad called us in?"

"A little. I felt a tiny bit . . . naughty."

"Same here."

She inches closer. "But I'm still here. It didn't deter me."

"Didn't deter me either." I swallow roughly. "With you, I'm not sure anything can."

She nibbles on her lips. "It's the same for me."

It's as if someone turned the thermostat to high. I'm burning up already, on fire for this woman. She scoots closer, threads a hand through my hair, scraping her nails across my scalp, delivering a jolt of lust straight to my groin. "Love that," I tell her.

Her eyes light up, blazing with desire as if I've said exactly the right thing. "Yeah?"

"You did it the other night, and it gets me going."

She hums, then does it again, dragging her nails through my hair. "I like turning you on."

"Then this ought to work out quite well for both of us."

She drops her mouth to my jaw, kissing me, making me groan. Climbing onto my lap, she straddles me. "So I'm dying to know," she murmurs, "what's the next course?"

I kiss the corner of her lips and tell her a little of what I have planned.

Her eyes sparkle with excitement. "I'm ready."

I run a finger under her bra strap. "Then I'm going to need to see the pink lingerie you're wearing. That strap has been driving me crazy all night. Why don't you get up and strip for me?"

She slides off me, ready and eager. And I'm pleased as hell that she's taking the lead right now.

30

Pink is definitely her color.

Then again, she looks good in anything. She looks great in nothing. She looks amazing taking everything off.

Standing in front of me in my living room, she slowly steps out of her heels. Unzips her jeans so deliberately it's torture. Shimmies them down her legs, making my mouth water.

Then she strips off her top, revealing herself in all her pink-lace beauty as I gaze at her from the couch where I'm enjoying the show.

"It's new," she says.

When she flicks her thumb over the candy-pink bra strap, I stand, stalk over to her, and run my hand down the lacy fabric of her bra. "Did you buy this for me?"

A coquettish jut of her hips is my first answer. Then a coy question: "What do you think?"

Sloane might have issues in the bedroom, but shyness is not one of them. She's definitely not lacking in the confidence department, nor the flirtation one either. She's bold, and it's outrageously enticing.

"Let's see," I answer as I slide my hand down to her waist, savoring the feel of her soft skin. "I bet you went shopping. I bet you looked for something incomparably sexy." My palm travels to her ass, cupping a cheek over the pink lace. "Maybe you even brought a friend along." My hand slinks lower, my fingers sliding along that fantastic line where her ass meets the top of her thigh. "Maybe you tried on a number of different lingerie sets. Am I getting warmer?"

Her shoulders rise and fall, and she lets out a smoky, sexy sigh. "I'd say you're getting hot. Getting *me* hot."

A groan rumbles up my chest as I let go of her ass, pressing a kiss to her neck and brushing her hair away. I slip my palm between her legs. *Heat.* So much delicious heat. The way she responds is a thing of beauty, a total high.

"That's how I want you," I tell her. "Hot. Wet. Aching."

"You've got me that way." Desire blazes in her brown eyes. "Do you like imagining me trying this on? Wondering how I looked in the dressing room?"

Our words are the first step in tonight's seduction. "I picture you in front of the mirror, gazing at your reflection, checking out how the bra pushes up your perfect tits. I bet you felt a rush of heat between your legs, knowing how much I'd want to rip these off you, knowing you'd drive me crazy looking like this."

She shudders against me, her breath coming in a rush. "Do I? Drive you wild?"

"What do you think?"

She darts out a hand, stroking my hard-on through my jeans, her lips curving into a deliciously self-satisfied grin. "Yes. *Wild.* I think that's a fair assessment."

I push against her palm as she strokes my length. "Now that we've established we're operating at off-the-charts levels of lust, there's something I want to make clear." I move my hands up her body until I'm holding her face.

"What is it?" A flicker of nerves crosses her brown eyes.

I shake my head, reassuring her. "Nothing you need to worry about. That's the thing. I don't want you to become obsessed with reaching the summit. I'm not saying you are. I just want you to feel good. Don't think about the orgasm. If you have one, great. If you don't, that's okay too."

"Are you sure?"

I smile. "Yes. I'm positive."

"But the other night you said you wanted me to have one."

"I know I said that, and I do want it, and you want it too." I stroke the backs of my fingers across her cheek. "But what I'm trying to say is let's take it as it goes. One moment at a time."

She leans into my touch like a cat. "I can do that."

"Don't focus on the endgame if you can help it. Enjoy the ride, and whatever happens, happens. Does that sound good?"

"It sounds great. No one's ever said that to me before."

I cringe for a second, hating that we have to bring the past into the conversation, but I know it's critical. "Has anyone ever tried to get you there? I mean, really tried?"

She shakes her head. "One guy tried to go harder, faster to get me there. Most didn't care that I hadn't come. The times I faked it, no one figured it out."

A part of me likes that she's never trusted anyone enough to tell them. Another piece wants to laugh at those poor schmucks for not even being able to add up the clues. Yet, another portion realizes what's most important. She's giving me the keys. She's never given them to anyone else.

"You've found someone who is obsessed with your pleasure. Let me show you what that's like." Taking her hand, I walk her to my bedroom, flick on the light, and bring her to my bed. She lies down, resplendent and decadent on my navy-blue comforter.

"You, in that pink bra with your waves of blonde hair and your big brown eyes and your smooth skin—you look like a perfect piece of candy on a summer day, and I want to lick you all over."

A shiver seems to run through her, like the prospect delights her senses. "Is that what you're going to do?"

"Tomorrow is for burying my face between your legs and tasting you coming on my tongue. Tonight we have other plans, and you know it." I head over to the nightstand. "You're not the only one who did a little shopping."

She sits up, eagerly clasping her hands. "What'd you get? What'd you get?"

After opening the drawer, I take out the gift I purchased for her. Her eyes widen when she sees the blue dolphin. "I figured we should set you up for success the first time."

"Are you going to fuck me with that toy?" She says each word like she thoroughly enjoys the filthy way they roll around on her tongue. That's yet another clue. Sloane wants to be unleashed. She wants to give in to abandon. She wants to feel everything she hasn't felt with a man before. And I'm the lucky bastard who gets to guide her there.

I drag the silicone head of the toy down her belly. "Yes, I'm going to fuck you hard with this vibrator. So hard and so good that you're going to grab the sheets, cry out in pleasure, and wonder how you're ever going to fuck yourself solo again. I'm going to make it that good."

She arches up against the toy and lets out the neediest groan. "I can't take it anymore. Just get me naked and do bad things to me."

31

When she puts it like that . . .

I slide down her panties, my breath evacuating from my lungs in a hot rush.

Shyly, almost demurely, she parts one leg only, like she's offering me a glimpse of the promised land. "We could take your pants off too, Dr. Goodman," she says.

"And will that turn you on even more?"

She slides a hand between her thighs, running a finger through her slickness, then offering it to me. "You tell me. Is it possible for me to be more turned on?"

Groaning with the intense need to touch, to taste, to have, I bring her finger to my lips and suck. My eyes roll back in my head, and I savor the sweet and salty taste of her. Pleasure rattles through me like a train barreling down the tracks, speeding around curves and blasting down the straightaway.

I let her finger fall from my lips then move to her bra, unclasping it and freeing her gorgeous tits.

And because the lady gets what the lady wants, I stand up to strip. "So you think this will get you going?" I tug off my pullover shirt, keeping my gaze on her as I go.

"Yes. So much yes."

When I pop open the button on my jeans, she slides her eager hand between her legs and starts playing.

I growl because it's so ridiculously sexy to see Sloane on my bed, naked, exploring her body. I shuck off my jeans and shed my boxer briefs, my cock springing free and greeting her with a proper salute.

She gasps, and her noise of appreciation is like a full day's injection of pride. She's seen me before, but the fact that she likes the view that much is everything my ego could ask for.

And maybe a little more.

I move to the top of the bed, stroking my cock once, twice, bringing a bead of liquid to the head.

She licks her lips, asking for it. I swipe the drop on my thumb, then run my thumb over her bottom lip. She moans obscenely, and I could come in seconds from those sexy sounds.

I reach for the dolphin and slide next to her, my hard length nestled against the soft, smooth flesh of her ass. "Spread your legs."

She does as asked. I drag the head of the toy between her legs, gliding it across all that slick, slippery wetness. She arches her back, bowing up against it instantly. She's like a violin, and I feel like a virtuoso already. I want to hear the music she can make. I want the symphony of her pleasure echoing across my bedroom. "Hold on to the headboard," I tell her.

She reaches up, clasping her hands around the slats. "Why?"

"It'll give you something to do with your hands."

She smiles at me. "Look at you, always thinking."

"So you don't have to. Just *feel*."

I rub the shaft across her center, getting her used to the feel, the size, the shape. If she's only ever come from a vibrator before, there's no need to pull out all the stops the first time around. My mission? Ease her into it. Get her there. Step by step. Orgasm by orgasm. I intend to build her up so that she can fall apart every single time with me.

"I want tonight to feel familiar to you. I want you to feel comfortable. To know you *can* get where you want to go. That's why I'm going to fuck you with this toy before we have sex again."

As she starts rubbing against the shaft, I turn on the dolphin head, sliding the buzzing nose against the delicious rise of her clit. The second, the very nanosecond that the toy makes contact, she lets out a primal groan.

It's long and needy. A plea for pleasure.

I heed it, stroking the toy against her. Sliding it up and down until she's writhing. When her breath turns uneven, when her hips lift faster, I slide it inside.

She groans as I go deeper, the sounds turning me on even more, and I didn't think it was possible to be more aroused. But hell, my dick is throbbing insistently against her lush body.

Sloane turns her gaze to me. Her eyes are rimmed with sex and lust. "That feels so good. I want you to fuck me so hard with it, Malone."

My temperature? It's forest-fire levels now. "That's exactly what I'm going to do."

I switch my position, moving to kneel between her legs and get a better angle.

"Yes." She lets out a guttural moan as she rocks against the vibrator. I follow her cues, fucking her with the toy. We quickly find a rhythm, a fast and feverish one. That's what this woman wants, and that's what I'm going to give her. She grips the headboard more tightly, her veins visible in her arms from the intensity. Her eyes squeeze shut, like she's chasing the edge of pleasure.

"You look so fucking sexy," I rasp as she grinds down on the toy.

"I feel sexy with you." Her words tumble from her lips, and if I were a betting man, I'd put all my money on the fact that Sloane is not thinking a goddamn thing right now.

She's feeling.

Feeling spectacular, I suspect.

She keeps rocking, thrusting her hips. "So good. God, it's sooooo good."

It's almost like she needs to say the words to

remind herself. Maybe so she doesn't get lost in her head again. Her legs fall open wider, her hips go wilder, her breath comes faster. Her lips part beautifully, and she murmurs.

Wanted you.

Wanted you to fuck me.

For so long.

Oh my God, for so long.

She seems to lose herself in the rhythm and the words. She can't seem to string them together, but she can't stop talking either, and it's an exquisite sight—Sloane losing her mind with impending ecstasy.

Wanted you.

Pictured you.

Harder.

Faster.

Yes, oh God, yes.

The sounds she makes are telltale. Her breath races. Her chest flushes pink. Her moans come from deep within her. Everything looks and feels so goddamn different from the other night. "Malone," she whispers, her voice breaking, wobbly. "Kiss me."

I don't need any greater command. I move up and seal my mouth to hers as I fuck her with the vibrator.

She shakes. She shudders. She trembles from head to toe. The kiss lasts all of five seconds because as soon as our lips touch, her mouth parts in an O. She falls silent, the quiet before the storm.

A small cry. A gasp. A whoosh of air.

She moans, her voice full of filthy wonder, rich with dirty joy. "I'm coming."

This.

This is the sexiest thing I've ever seen. Sloane, losing control, for real.

Coming undone with me, for me.

As her voice breaks and she hits that high, I know with a crisp certainty that I want to do this to her again and again.

I can't get enough of this woman.

* * *

Soon enough, she comes down from her orgasm, her eyes flickering open, looking sex-drunk and happy as a cat stretching in the sunniest spot in the house.

Slowly, I ease the toy out of her, setting it on the bed.

"Thank you," she whispers, and it sounds full of reverence, as if I've given her a great gift.

"All I did was hit the on button," I say with a playful shrug.

Letting go of the headboard, she sits up and grabs my face. "That was everything. You made me feel like I was flying. Like I was free. Like I could let go and give in. I've never felt that . . . open."

Holy hell.

I'm king of the world.

She makes me feel ten feet tall.

She slides her hand down my body. Her soft hand

on my hard cock is too much. It's going to unravel me, make me lose all willpower.

But we aren't going there yet.

I shake my head, removing her hand. "We're not having sex."

"Please." She wiggles against me, and I nearly surrender. I'm ready to throw my plans out the window just to get inside her.

But that'd be selfish. I can't stick my dick inside her to get off.

When I sleep with her again, I need to believe I can send her soaring. "We need more practice. I want to make you come in every other way first."

She pouts, then drags a hand up her belly, tracing a seductive path along her flesh. Stopping between her tits, she plays with a hard nipple. "You don't have to put your cock *inside* me."

My mouth goes dry as she slides her other hand between her legs, stroking a few times before she brings it between her breasts, coating them with the evidence of her own orgasm. "Why don't you fuck me here?"

I'm a lightning bolt of lust.

What am I going to say to that but *hell to the fucking yes?*

In no time, I straddle her, slide my hand between her legs to gather more of the goodness, then slick some along my cock. She pushes her breasts together, and I jerk forward, sliding my length between those gorgeous globes.

It's the most perfect valley, and when her tits cradle my dick, I'm sure, I'm positively fucking sure, it's not going to take me long at all.

Because I'm a gentleman, I give her a warning. "This is going to be pretty fast."

She lifts her face, her lips all swollen and sexy. "Come quickly. Come slowly. Just come on me."

True to my word, I'm nearly there already. A couple of thrusts, a couple of strokes, and my already aching dick is singing a happy tune, ready to blast off. My vision blurs, and my world spirals into pure bliss as I come on her chest.

The release is exhilarating and exactly what I need.

I shudder, grunting her name, grunting God's name, panting hard. She reaches down, drags a finger between her breasts, and shoots me a naughty stare as she licks her fingertip. "Maybe I just wanted to be a dirty girl."

"You picked the right guy. Now let's clean you up." I take her to the shower, and I wash her off. She seems to savor the attention, and it makes me realize there's nothing at all wrong with her.

Sure, she might think too much.

Yeah, her brain can get in the way of her body's wishes.

But maybe that's because she hasn't found the right person to give her everything she deserves.

Or hasn't until now.

32

I turn off the shower and hand her a towel.

As she dries, she casually says, "Once I'm all dressed, I can go."

I rub my ear. "What did you just say?"

She shrugs as if it's no big deal, then points to the door. "I figured you'd want me to go."

"Why the hell would you figure that?"

"Because that's . . ."

"What guys want?" I supply, aghast. "Who the hell have you been dating?" I hold up a hand. "Wait. I'm not sure I want you to answer that."

"I didn't want to be presumptuous." She's too direct and up-front to beg or even hint for an invite. No, she legit sounds like she thought I'd kick her out of my home after pleasuring her. "You might want your space," she says. "We didn't make any plans for an all-nighter."

I slide a hand around her hip, squeezing. "You

might not be presumptuous, but I sure as hell am. You're not coming over here, having dinner with me, wearing that sexy-as-sin pink lingerie, having an epic orgasm that we both desperately wanted, showering in my bathroom, and then getting in a cab, Uber, or subway *to go home.*" I squeeze harder. "If I'm presumptuous, so be it. You're spending the night. Got it?"

A smile spreads slowly over her lovely face, then all at once, as if she's been lit up. "That's crystal clear."

I let go of her hip and tuck a finger under her chin. "Besides, do I look like some kind of Neanderthal? A twenty-two-year-old Tinder hookup? A jackass frat guy?"

She laughs and shakes her head. "No. But . . ."

I shake my head, still in a fog of disbelief. "All right. I have to ask: Do you have a thing for assholes? Are you one of those women who likes to date jerks?"

She smirks. "No. I swear. But . . ."

"But you've wound up with some dickheads?"

She shrugs. "It's been known to happen to women in their twenties. Look, I haven't always picked well. I meet men at the gym or through dating apps or even in my online groups for small business owners selling stuff on Etsy, like the socks I sell. And I went out with a couple of guys who were the poster boys for the classic girl questions of *Does he like me? Why doesn't he text? Is he just busy?*"

I shake my head, running the towel once over my hair then tossing it on a hook. "Let me tell you something. We're never too busy to text. It's not complicated to send a quick note." I mime tapping with thumbs. "*Yo, girl, what's up?* See? Two seconds. Now, giving a dog a new ACL? That takes time. Stitching up a cat who broke her leg? That's precision work. Sending a woman you dig a text is a pleasure and don't let anyone tell you differently."

She taps my chest. "And when we like a guy, we like hearing from him. Also, I like it when you text me, and then we wind up having long conversations. But then, that's what always happens with us."

"That's the truth," I say, and for one moment, awareness flashes before my eyes.

We're talking like we're together.

I'm telling her everything. The secrets of men. The truth of our behavior. How I feel.

But we can't be together.

Our reality isn't going away—she's my business partner's daughter. She's been branded off-limits. And there's a new obstacle too—the whole working-in-the-same-space one. It's simply too risky to test the limits. We need to be able to treat patients and run the clinic without awkwardness or tension.

This, the way we are at night, is our alternate universe.

Maybe that's why we can be so open here. We can enjoy this tryst for what it is: a second time around in our parallel world.

But the end will come just the same.

That thought weighs me down, and I don't want to be anyplace but up tonight. Time to stow all the worries and the obstacles. Resolved, I set them on a mental shelf and close the door for the night.

I step closer to Sloane. "Plus, you can't leave with wet hair." Gently, I take her towel and rub it over her head, drying the ends of her hair as I speak. "You're getting in my bed, and you're spending the night naked and curled up in my arms. We'll probably even chat for a few minutes. We might even blow each other's minds again."

She hums. "Now you're talking."

We return to the bedroom and flop onto the bed. I brush my fingertips along her waist. "So, tell me about your socks."

She laughs. "I'm not even wearing any tonight," she says, wiggling her bare feet.

"I know. And trust me, it makes me really sad, because the thought of you in nothing but a pair of socks is a turn-on."

She arches one brow, giving me a curious look. "That turns you on?"

I glance down at my dick. He's showing off his two-seconds-to-semi skills again. "Apparently. I'm not sure if you've gotten the message yet. But everything you do turns me on."

She shifts to her side, facing me, propping her head in her hand. "If I took off a sock, that would turn you on?" She mimes removing one sock.

I pretend to consider that scenario. "Yep."

"If I have a drink of water, that would turn you on?" She pretends to down a glass.

I do a slow, exaggerated nod. "Absolutely. Major wood."

She checks me out, her eyes indicating she's impressed. I don't lie—I'm at full mast again.

"If I open a bottle of ketchup, would that be arousing?"

I quirk up my lips, considering. "Yeah. I'm pretty sure it would. You could also eat an apple, and that would be enticing. You could walk down the hallway, and that would be stimulating. You could yawn, and I'd probably be ready to go."

She shoves her hand against my chest. "You're so easy."

I pinch her butt. "What can I say? You do it for me, Sloane. You can test it with a sock striptease, but it's true. I'm an easy mark with you."

She slides up against me, grinning. "And do you think I'm easy with you?"

A cough bursts from my throat. "You? Easy? Not in the least."

"Hey!"

I draw a line down her nose. "If turning you on was a simple task, you wouldn't be in my bed, getting lessons in orgasms."

"And I do like my lessons. I'm a good student, don't you think?"

"You take direction incredibly well."

"I can relax with you. Being with you like this . . . is easy." Her tone softens, downshifts to vulnerable.

climax, but it also helps you be present in your body. Can we see if that works?"

I wiggle my fingers. "I love the way you think. Let's try it now."

She presses her beautiful naked body against mine. "I'm up for it."

"I'm definitely up for it."

Soon enough, she's fucking my fingers, closing her eyes, and, I imagine, seeing stars.

As it should be.

In the morning, after she leaves, I find a note from her on my fridge.

33

Sloane Elizabeth's Notes to Malone

Top Five Things I Like About You

One: You're a good listener.

Two: Your restaurant-ordering skills are unparalleled.

Three: Your dick.

Four: Your confidence. You knew I was going to mention your cock, didn't you? How could I not? It's glorious. It's big and pretty and perfect.

Four and a half: Your comfort in your own skin.

Because even if I didn't mention your cock, you'd have been fine with that.

Five: Your eyes. They melt me every time you look my way.

Six: The way you make me laugh.

Seven: The way you take things seriously, and then you don't take things seriously at all.

Eight: How much you love animals.

Nine: Your determination.

Ten: The fact that you have way more than five things to list.

Eleven: And way more than ten too.

34

On my way to work out the next morning, I hum a tune.

"You're always wishing and wanting for something."

Isn't that the truth? There is so damn much I want. *"When you get what you want, you don't want what you get."*

Oh, but I do want it, Irving Berlin. I want it badly.

The sex and everything else. Last night was more than a good screw.

Last night made me see there are so many things for my top five list too. But, like her, I can't keep myself to just five. That's the trouble. Sloane is thoughtful and bighearted. She loves animals and wants to save them all. She talks to the kitties who need company, and she made friends with Sam on the first day in the clinic. She cares about her parents and looks out for her friends. She gave me a Frank Sinatra bootleg CD—one she tracked down in record time because she knew I was salivating for it.

The woman is an angel and a goddess.

And then there's the pièce de résistance: She lets me in. She opens up. She shares herself.

If I don't watch out, I'm going to fall flat on my ass for her.

Good thing I'm seeing my buddy Herb for a quick round of basketball before work, since time with him tends to keep me chill—he's a laid-back guy. We catch up on the court in our game of one-on-one.

"And how are all the pampered poodles and teacup Chihuahuas on the Upper East Side doing?" I ask as I shoot.

"They're all coming to me, so I can't complain. Business is booming, and it's nice to be the one calling the shots."

"I bet it is," I say, a slight pang of envy stabbing me. Herb's been running his own practice for a few years, and he's absolutely loving it.

"You'll get there soon enough." He sends the ball soaring, and it drops gracefully through the net. "Besides, don't you have enough complications at work right now?"

I scoff as I grab the rebound, grateful he knows the basics about Sloane and I don't have to explain them anew. "That's a safe way of putting it."

I'll just have to keep taking each day as it comes.

I say goodbye, head home for a quick shower, then walk to work.

Before my mind wanders back to thoughts of Sloane tangled up in my sheets, or forward to all those knotty complications at work, I call my mom. We catch up on daily life, with her sharing details on Cole and Porter, and me telling her about work.

"And how is it with Doug still being there?"

I maintain a chipper attitude. "I'm managing just fine. What's one more year? I'm sure Dad would understand."

"Darling, your father would be proud of you if you never owned your own practice," she says firmly.

"I know, but I still want to. It means a lot to me."

"And I'm proud of you too," she adds, pressing her point. "You've done a lot with your life already. You're true to your name. You're a good man, and you've been a great junior partner with Doug. I'm sure he values you immensely, so hold on to that.'"

And maybe calling my mom wasn't the best idea. Now I'm thinking of all the ways Doug might *not* value me if he knew I'd crossed the line.

I thank her and head into the clinic; say a quick hello to Jonathan and Sam, who are bent over at her desk, laughing at something on her phone; and then meet with Doug to review a study I've been working on. He puts on his glasses, reads my notes, and then says, "Damn, it's as if I've trained you well. This is perfect."

I beam, pleased that the man still respects my work. I return to the front to check out the appointment list for the day, but at the edge of the room, I stop in my tracks.

Jonathan is leaning close to Sam. His hand is on her back. This is a brand-new level of connection between them. "We should go out again tonight," he says softly.

Their backs are to me. "Do you want to go to that pub quiz at the Grouchy Owl?" she asks.

"Yeah. That sounds awesome." His hand brushes her back, touching the ends of her hair before he turns around.

When he sees me, his eyes widen into an *oh shit* expression. I offer a smile. "I definitely think you guys should do the trivia quiz. Also, the Grouchy Owl has great live music."

Sam winces. "Are we in trouble?"

"Shoot, man. I'm sorry," Jonathan jumps in.

"Why are you guys sorry? It sounds like you're having a fun time together. Though, admittedly, I was hoping you were using the movie gift certificates," I say.

Sam offers a sheepish smile. "This weekend."

Jonathan shoots me a guilty expression. "There's probably a rule against this. No fraternizing. We were trying to keep it quiet."

I clap his shoulder. "It's all good. There are no rules. Our office is too small for that. And besides, who would make rules like that? I'm just glad it's going well for you guys."

I head to my office, snickering, and Sloane pops in

for a minute, clicking the door shut. "Is there something in the air at your office? I was bringing you some forms for a doctor's signature and I overheard."

"Clearly, there's some kind of hookup dust here in this office."

"Either that or there's something in the water." She taps her chin. "Maybe I should have another glass."

"While you're at it, I'll take a double," I joke.

She's quiet for a minute, then quirks up her lips. "Do you want to go out tonight?"

"To the Grouchy Owl? I like Jonathan and Sam, but I'm not ready to double with my employees."

She shakes her head. "Someplace else. *Something* else. Before the main event."

"Ah, I wonder, wonder, wonder what I have planned on the tour of O-ville tonight," I say, tapping my chin, mirroring her gesture.

She smiles in appreciation. "Why don't you work on the Summit Town tour activities, and I'll plan something for us to do before? Because I was thinking how seductive it was to have dinner and listen to Frank together last night before you began your Orgasm Sherpa work."

I lean back in my chair, park my hands behind my head, and prop my feet on the desk. For effect, of course. "That was all part of my role, Sloane. But by all means, feel free to sherpa me tonight."

Her eyes twinkle. "I plan to."

She spins around on her heel and leaves.

Maybe something *is* in the air here.

It makes me start to wonder. To wonder how to have something I shouldn't.

As I move through the day treating patients, I start to imagine another alternate universe.

One where we aren't just going to Tahiti for a week.

Fact is, I'm dying to know what she has planned tonight, but she doesn't need to seduce me. She already has.

That feels like a good thing, but it's a hell of a problem too.

35

She waits for me at the Lincoln Center fountain, perched on the stone edge, the water arcing behind her in moonlit choreography.

Her foot swings back and forth, a red high-heeled shoe drawing me like a beacon. My eyes drink up the view of her blonde hair cascading down her bare shoulders, her light-blue dress both hinting at and hiding the lush body that lies beneath. She's never been flashy in her clothes—she always shows just enough to light my imagination.

As I walk toward her, her eyes stroll up and down my frame, giving me the same treatment I did her: a comprehensive checking out. Good thing I'm dressed the way she likes me best—tailored slacks, a dress shirt, and a tie.

It also helps that I can follow instructions like it's my fucking job, since she texted me and told me the attire.

When I reach her, she gives me a final survey then a low, appreciative whistle. Standing, she reaches for my tie and yanks me in close with it. "You look hot as hell," she says, and before I can even murmur a thank you, she claims me.

She kisses me hard. Possessively. Blotting out all the patrons at Lincoln Center. Hell, she erases the rest of the city as she consumes my lips and turns my body white-hot.

I cup her cheek, clasp her face, and kiss her back with the same ferocity. When we separate, she wobbles, and I steady her, reaching for her elbow.

"Why, yes, I do believe we're on the express train to Summit Town tonight," she murmurs.

Laughing, I drape an arm around her and gesture to the buildings that house the arts. "And I'll be your conductor. But first, sherpa me."

She leans her shoulder against mine, smiling. "The place I had in mind is about fifteen blocks away. On Amsterdam. I just wanted to meet here because I like these fountains."

I glance at the sprays of water tangoing brightly behind us. "They're quite romantic."

Her eyes widen and her tone is laced with worry. "Is that bad?"

My brow knits. "No. Not at all. Why would that be bad?"

She fidgets with her earring. "Just didn't want to imply anything."

Is the idea of romance anathema to her? Is she

against relationships? Maybe she's so damn focused on work and her rescue she's not even thinking of romance. Hell, maybe I'm the only one who's let his mind wander down that path.

Then I kick myself.

You're not going to have a romance with her. You work with her father. You work with her. It doesn't matter how easy Jonathan and Sam make it seem to have an office relationship. That doesn't mean a romantic relationship will work for you. The only romance you should be thinking of is the kind that's part of the seduction. That kind is one of the key tools to help her reach the peak. You're her guide.

Just guide her.

I run my fingers over a few strands of her hair. "The fountains are beautiful. And you looked even prettier framed by them." There's some romance for her, safely couched as a compliment. We walk down the steps. "Now tell me about the place you've picked for tonight."

"I think you're going to love it. I asked Piper for advice—she's an elite wedding planner, and she knows everything about the city. She said there's a great underground lounge with hipster drinks and red curtains and purple couches that looks like something you'd find in a New Orleans speakeasy, and there's an up-and-coming singer named Delilah who puts the torch in torch singer. She'll be performing tonight."

"What does she sing?"

"Billie. Linda. Norah. You'll love her."

I hum my enthusiasm. "Linda. Damn, woman. Now you're taking *me* to O Town."

She laughs. "I had a feeling you might like Linda Ronstadt."

"And I'm man enough to admit it to anyone." We reach the crosswalk and stop.

She shoots me a saucy look, her eyes narrowing. "Do it. Proclaim your love for Linda."

I scoff. "Please. That's easy." I hold my hands out wide, turning 180 degrees and shouting loud and proud, "Linda Ronstadt is a goddess."

A guy across the block with a hoodie and a knit cap gives a rocker salute. "Right back at you, man."

An older woman laden with a canvas bag bursting with books pats my elbow. "Bless your heart. A young man with taste is a rare breed these days."

"Thank you," I say with a smile.

"He does have great taste," Sloane adds. "He's a Sinatra man too."

The woman raises her salt-and-pepper eyebrows. "If he's good in bed and treats you right, then you should keep him."

The lady turns the corner, leaving her wisdom wafting in the evening breeze.

Sloane whips her gaze to me, a hint of a smile crossing her lips. I'm not entirely sure where to go after that last comment, so I sidestep it. "Looks like I just launched an impromptu Linda Ronstadt fan club."

Sloane follows my lead. "And you have so many

charter members already. By the way, count me in. 'I Don't Stand a Ghost of a Chance with You' is a favorite tune of mine."

The reference isn't lost on me. We kissed to that song seven years ago. Kissed to the whole damn number. I hum a few words as we walk.

She squeezes my arm. "If you do that . . ."

"If I do that, what?"

"I'm going to jump you."

Laughing, I add a few more lines, a little louder, a little deeper this time. She runs her hand down my arm. "It's your fault I'm aroused."

I hold up my hands in surrender. "I fully take the blame."

"Hey!" She stops walking and grabs my arms. "You should record an album."

I laugh it off. "Please."

"No, you should. Do it for fun. It's an adventure. Put something together. And then everyone can swoon the way I do."

"You want to share me?" I tease.

"That's the only part of you I want to share. But look at it this way—you could help couples everywhere. Your voice is total sex."

And as I hum a few more lines to her, she's like a cat, rubbing against me.

When we reach the club, she tugs me close and whispers, "You were warned."

We make our way down a wooden staircase, below ground level, and find a velvet couch. Sloane slides in next to me and is all hands on my legs and fingers in my hair for the next hour. It's distracting and heady as she whispers sweet nothings in my ear. As she tells me she wants me. As she tells me how good I am to her.

I'm buzzed, I'm drunk, I'm wildly aroused.

With Sloane's busy fingers and constant touches, I barely hear a word Delilah sings.

Nor do I care.

I'm nothing but an electrical line, charged and ready.

I'm not sure who's seducing who. But from the way she kisses my neck and slides her hand along my pants, I think she's leading me up the mountain tonight. I have the idea, too, that the more she leads, the harder I'll fall.

The more I'll be the one wanting the romance.

The more I'll be the one singing the love songs about the one who got away.

Singing it and meaning it.

That's the problem.

My jaw tightens as reality inches back in, undeniable.

I'm falling for her.

Yet again.

By the time the singer finishes "Guess I'll Hang My Tears Out to Dry," I desperately need to go. I need to reframe this night, put the focus back on sex and seduction.

If I stay in this club, with these songs and her

sweetness, I'll be a sad, pathetic jerk begging her to stay with me for another week, then another.

That's not our deal.

I call a Lyft, and the whole ride downtown, I take control, whispering to Sloane all the things I want to do to her when we get inside. I tell her how I want to touch her, taste her, strip her down to nothing. By the time we make it to my apartment, she looks like she's hovering on the edge.

I intend to send her all the way to the other side.

That's what I need right now.

To recalibrate *us* back to pleasure and pleasure only.

36

She's all fire and heat.

The second we're inside my place, she pushes me to the door, slamming me against it.

I growl at her roughness, loving it.

She growls back, rubbing up against me, grinding her pelvis to mine.

The first night we were together, I slowed her down. But this time, I let her have her way. There's no need to tap the brakes tonight, because I understand now what she's driving toward.

This is how she blots out her overactive brain. She quiets the noise with intensity. She seeks a fevered kind of contact because it leaves room for only that in her head.

Pleasing her isn't about possessing a magical penis or a special-powered tongue. It's as simple as listening to the woman's cues. Judging from the way her hands hurriedly roam up and down my arms, touching, seeking, squeezing, she might need to be in charge for a while. I'm man enough to let her lead when she needs to.

She tugs at my shirt, yanking it from my pants. "You. I want you," she gasps. "It's so good with you. Like it's never been with anyone else."

Best. Words. Ever.

"Same for me," I mutter as the heat intensifies, sizzling over my skin.

But soon, with her mind-bending kisses, her greedy touches, my restraint unravels. I thread my hand into her hair and yank it back, tugging hard. Bringing my mouth down on her neck, I suck and I bite. She moans and writhes against me, grabbing at the buttons on my shirt, trying desperately to undo them.

"Just rip it off," I tell her.

With wide eyes, she stares at me, dirty delight in them. "Really?"

I nod savagely. "You know you want to."

"I do." She pulls, tearing the buttons down.

Ping. Ping. Ping.

They clatter to the floor. Sensual glee spreads in her brown irises as she inhales sharply. "I've always wanted to do that," she says.

That's the operative word. *Want.*

I tug her hair, travel up her neck, and bite her earlobe. "I think the issue isn't in your head, sweetheart."

She breathes out hard. "What do you mean?"

"Maybe you haven't *wanted* anyone enough to come. Maybe you haven't felt enough of this kind of red-hot desire to let go the way you need to."

She slides her palm between us, grappling at my erection. "I want you that much, Malone. I want to let go with you."

"Tell me what you want tonight. Tell me what you're desperate to do."

She raises her hands, grabs my face, and holds me roughly. "I want to ride your face."

A groan tears through me, pure lust rushing to every single molecule. "Then get naked and get on me."

In the bedroom, our clothes come off in a mad flurry, and we're on the bed, crawling toward the headboard, tangled up in each other. I slide underneath her, grabbing her hips. "Fuck my face, Sloane. Do it however you want. Fast, slow, rough, hard."

She lowers herself to me, and I bring her down to my mouth. I groan against her pussy, so wet, so ready, so damn eager.

She cries out at that first touch, at the very moment we make contact. I lick a line up her center, flick my tongue against her hard clit, and suck her like I'm kissing her fiercely. She shudders and lets out a sound so carnal, so feral that it gets me even harder, and it makes her even wetter. She falls forward, grabbing at the headboard.

For a moment, I break contact, whispering

roughly, "Show me how much you want me, Sloane. Fuck my face that way."

That's all she needs. The freedom to be who she is, and she's off, rocking and riding and finding the angle, the speed, the pace that she needs. The taste of her is intoxicating, the scent divine. Her sounds are a filthy symphony, making my dick ache.

The amount of lust in my body is more than one man can sustain. With one hand on her hip, I slide the other down to grip my cock, fisting it. The relief is temporary, but so damn necessary.

I stroke and jerk as she rocks and swivels, her noises intensifying, her groans growing, and her moves turning ever more frantic. She glances behind her and gasps.

Oh God.

That's so . . .

You.

Hot.

Malone.

Do it.

Get yourself off.

I grip my cock as she goes crazy on my face. She's off like a shot, as if discovering my lust has flipped the switch.

Her taste floods my tongue; her sounds echo through the room. I let go of my grip on my shaft, clutching her hips so she doesn't fall as she shakes and shudders against me. But when she comes down from her high, she's a cheetah, scrambling. She's between my legs in a flash.

Everything is a blur.

Her mouth on me.

Sucking.

Licking.

Cupping me.

Her hair spilling all over my legs. Her noises. My own groans and moans. She's gripping, licking, sucking, and then my orgasm obliterates my mind, racing down my body till I'm coming hard in her mouth, grabbing her hair, grunting and growling. *"Yes. Fuck. Yes."*

Shudders wrack my body, and I come for days.

After, she curls up against me. "Do you know what did it for me?"

I know. But she wants to say it, so I ask, "What did it for you?"

"Seeing you touch yourself," she answers, teasing her fingers along my belly.

"Yeah?"

She nods. "That's one of the best things I'm learning from these lessons."

It's a warm glow, the knowledge that this experience has become more enlightening than either one of us expected. We're both discovering things about each other. We're experiencing more than the fast track to coming. "What are you learning exactly?"

Absently, she drags her fingers up and down my pecs.

"I didn't know this when we started. But now, I think what I was missing all along was to *want* somebody this much. To want someone the way I want you. That's my biggest turn-on. That's what keeps me in the zone."

I'm back in the zone already. "That's the hottest thing anyone has ever said to me."

She grins. "And then to look down and see you getting yourself off, to know you were so turned on that you simply *had* to touch yourself—that sent me soaring. That's what turns me on more than anything."

I slide a hand through her hair, my skin buzzing. "Sloane, there is nothing sexier than you chasing your pleasure." There's something I want to say. Something I'm realizing. "You know, you're not the only one learning here."

"Is that so?"

"These last few nights—they don't feel like lessons. Or not like I'm giving you lessons. It feels like we're both listening to each other. Paying attention to each other."

"It does feel that way. Like I'm figuring out how you like it too."

I stage-cough. "I like it every way with you."

"But I like knowing that. And I like how wild you get when you're near the end. You're loud and rough, and I love getting you there."

"And I've learned that you have a tiger in you."

She laughs, then affects a roar. "Maybe I do."

I run my hand down her belly. "Maybe you just needed someone to let the tiger come out and play."

She pretends to purr. "Do tigers purr?"

I shake my head. "No. The only big cat that can purr is the cheetah. Smaller cats purr, like bobcats, cougars, and house cats."

"Now this does feel like a lesson," she says, deadpan. "A science lesson."

I laugh and tickle her sides. "You asked, woman."

"Stop, stop," she cries out.

I relent, and she sighs happily then lifts her eyebrows and makes a rumbling sound, imitating a very content pussycat.

"Fine," I say. "The female of the genus Vixenus Sloane can also purr." I flip her to her back and kiss her stomach. "But only when fucked properly by the one man who knows how to turn her into a complete pussycat."

Her purr grows louder. "You do make me purr."

"That's the goal, woman. That's always the goal."

She straightens, raising herself higher, meeting my eyes intently. She swallows, as if she's prepping to say something hard. "Maybe that's the magic touch. Maybe you're the magic."

That warm glow? It winds through me, touching down in every corner, filling me with something bigger, something stronger, more intense.

Perhaps it's the orgasm affecting my brain.

Maybe great sex can loosen lips.

Though there's so much more going on between

us than great sex. And part of me—a big part of me—doesn't want to play the parallel universe game any longer.

Whether she wants romance or not, I need to say this. Let it out for the sake of my own heart, which has grown two sizes too big with her.

I kiss her gently and speak the full and terrifying truth. "No. *We're* the magic. Together."

Her eyes lock with mine, her brown gaze big and vulnerable. I wait, wondering, hoping she feels that way. "I believe that, Malone."

That's my greatest wish and my greatest worry. That we are too right for each other. Too good together. I feel too much. I want too much. I need her too much.

And what do I do with all these emotions?

How can we possibly find a way through?

Unless . . .

What if I've been wrong about not being able to have her? What if there's a way to navigate around the roadblocks, to jump over the hurdles?

What if we can figure it all out?

I don't know that route to a relationship like I do the one to her pleasure. But I want to find it. I *have* to find it.

She snuggles against me, yawning, and starts to drift off in my arms. First, though, she asks in a sleepy, sexy voice, "When are you going to make love to me?"

I close my eyes, squeezing them shut, knowing

that's what it will be. And I whisper against her neck, "The next time we're together."

The trouble is, I don't know how I'll ever come back from that.

Or if I want to. I want to move forward and I need to find a way to do that because I don't want to give her up a second time.

37

It's a pancakes kind of morning.

"When I ran into you the other week, you offered me pancakes, and now I'm taking you up on it," Sloane declares when we get out of the shower.

"It's about time."

"But I'm going to need a sweatshirt or something, so I don't look like I'm doing a total walk of shame."

My eyes take a quick tour of her body, enjoying the post-shower look. "Maybe next time, you should bring a change of clothes. More than just panties," I tell her as she grabs a pair of white undies from her purse and tugs them on, then slips on her dress.

Her eyes light up as if she likes the idea. "Maybe next time I will."

Next time, next time, next time.

All I want are more times with her.

She pulls on a gray sweatshirt from my alma

mater, and we head to the diner around the corner, where I spot my buddy Herb and his fiancée, Olivia.

She waves to me from their booth and he holds up a hand to say hi.

"We just ordered. Want to join us"?" Olivia asks.

Sloane shrugs happily. "Sounds good." She extends a hand, and I quickly make introductions.

"Herb's a vet too. He's the king of the Upper East Side."

Herb squares his shoulders. "That is true. I had a new sign made up for my practice that says just that."

Olivia turns to Sloane. "How is your rescue doing? I saw the video of Malone singing to the cat and followed it to your page. Looks like you're doing great things."

Sloane flashes a smile. "We are. At least I think so. We've adopted out fourteen animals in the last two weeks, and my foster network is expanding. Having a reliable office space to run it makes a big difference. I was using a spot in Brooklyn, but the rent went up, so I feel lucky to have a place at all, and being able to easily manage all the animal care is huge. Well, thanks to Malone."

"And your dad," I add.

She chuckles. "Yes, but let's be honest. You're doing most of the work."

"True . . ." I admit. Doug's around a bit more, but the bulk of the work still falls to me.

Olivia jumps in, gesturing to Sloane. "By the way, Malone's sweatshirt looks nice on you."

I roll my eyes, ready to defend her attire.

Sloane plucks at the gray fabric. "This thing? Yeah. It might as well say *walk of shame.*"

Olivia holds up a hand to high-five. "Own it, girl."

Sloane smiles. "It's worth a ten-mile walk if I have to."

Herb's eyes widen, and he high-fives me. "That's downright impressive."

I preen, damn glad we made a pit stop here.

Sloane slides right into the chitchat with my friends.

This is how it could be.

This is what I could have.

This is what I want.

I try to shake away those notions when we leave, but they linger, chasing me as I put her in a cab and tell her I'll see her at the office later.

They follow me as I head into work, saying hi to Jonathan and Sam, who are deep in conversation.

"And listen, if your mom gives you a hard time, just tell her you damn well know how to decorate your own apartment," he says to her.

"You're right. That's what I'm going to say."

I smile inside at how easy they make it seem. They've slipped so seamlessly into being together, they make it look like walking on air.

Inside my office, I pick up the photo of my dad. "What would you do?"

The thing is, I think I know. I just wish I had another opinion.

But I put the question aside as I get to work on the day's spays and neuters. I can't have anything on my mind but snipping and clipping.

When I'm done, I blot my forehead with my sleeve, wash my hands, and take a deep breath.

I should call Truly. See her tonight. Ask for advice.

I've turned toward my office to make a call, when Doug strides out of an exam room, saying goodbye to the last patient of the day.

He tips his chin in my direction. "Do you have a few minutes to chat?"

My heart drops, and guilt washes over me in a hot wave.

He knows.

He's found out.

And I'm about to be fucked.

38

Sloane Elizabeth's Notes to Self on ALL THE THINGS

Let's review the facts as we know them.

Your father wants to talk.

Your father specifically said he has something he wants to discuss with you and Malone.

You're sleeping with Malone.

Don't even try to deny it on a technicality. You slept with him, and you intend to sleep with him again, and you'd like to sleep with him every single night from now until eternity because you're wild about him.

But there's that little matter of working in close quarters with him.

And then there's the bigger matter of banging your dad's business partner.

Your dad is either going to kick your rescue out of his office space and tell you you're a trollop, or he'll say he isn't mad, just disappointed.

All of which suck.

Chin up, girl. Put on your best socks.

39

Doug is imperious, perched in his chair, positioned behind his desk, his face impassive.

My stomach plummets all the way to my feet, which have turned cold and heavy like concrete.

There are no two ways to spin this. He's my business partner, and I've been screwing his daughter.

He could yank the rug out from under me, toss me to the street, and slam the door closed.

I love this clinic. I love the clients and the patients and the employees, and yet I've been thinking with my little head.

I drag my concrete feet to the chair in front of his desk and sit. A second later, Sloane walks in. "Hi, Dad."

She sounds as if she's doing her damnedest to stay strong, not to let on that she did the walk of shame earlier today.

But he has to know, or why call us in here?

"Shut the door, please," he says coolly.

She shuts it with a dull thud before taking the chair next to mine.

Doug folds his hands. "I should have arranged a dinner or done this outside of work, but it's about Helena."

I blink. That's not what I expected. I sit up straighter.

Sloane leans forward. "Is she okay, Daddy?" Worry threads through her tone, and in this instant, I see her fully as his daughter. She's his anxious child, concerned about his wife, calling him "Daddy."

Doug clasps his hand to his chest. "She's great. Didn't mean to scare you. She's the picture of health."

Slumping back in the chair, Sloane lets out a deep sigh. "Don't talk like that, then. You had me terrified she was sick."

Doug's face turns ashen. "No, God no. She's great. Thank the Lord." He pauses. "But she is worried sick about me."

"Why?" I ask. "Are *you* okay?"

He thumps his fist on his sternum. "Fit as a fiddle."

"That sounds like a good thing, Doug." I keep my voice steady because now I have no clue what's going on. "Why is she worried?"

"Here's the deal. Remember when I asked you where you thought I should take Helena on vacation?" he says to Sloane.

"Yes, and I suggested you ask her what her dream vacation was," Sloane supplies.

"And I did just that. I asked her. Want to know what she said?"

I'm dying to. I'm still in the goddamn dark.

Doug holds his hands out wide, then a smile spreads slowly across his face. "She wants to go to Europe. For three months. Maybe more. She wants *us* —her and me—to go. Because she's worried I work too much. And you know what I said?"

I narrow my brow. "No?"

He laughs, shaking his head and reaching into his desk drawer. He grabs a red beret, positions it jauntily on his head, and says, *"Mais oui,"* in his best French accent.

"You're leaving?" I ask, incredulous. Is he for real?

"Yes. Well, I hope you don't mind. But I need to do this. What the woman wants, the woman gets. And she wants me in Europe, and she has to be the priority." He gestures to me, earnest and open. "Honestly, you do most of the work here anyway. So I thought I'd just take some time off and let you two run it."

I freeze.

Run it?

He wants the two of us to manage the clinic?

"Excuse me?" Sloane asks, shock coloring her tone.

He looks at his daughter. "I thought you two could keep the ship running while I go. You've been operating the rescue out of here, and it's going great. The practice is running smoothly, thanks to Malone. If you can pick up a little of the slack on the business side for me, that would be great. Any business decisions I would've had a hand in if I were here, I know you can handle." He looks to both of us now. "And all you have to do is keep working together like the pros that you are, and it'll be fine, right? Surely no one will miss me that much. I've been cutting back anyway."

"But you're still the partner?" I ask carefully, since I got ahead of myself last time, hoping he was about to hand me the keys.

"Of course. I'm not ready to sell it. But you'll collect the profits since you'll be doing the veterinary work. The practice is yours to run." He turns to Sloane. "And you can keep running the rescue out of the clinic too, and the pair of you can make the bulk of the decisions. It's gone well with you working in tandem so far." He beams. "This will work out perfectly."

I'm not so sure about that.

* * *

After Doug leaves, I head to my office, trying to process what just happened. The clinic is closed for the night, and Jonathan and Sam are gone, probably partaking of pizza and a movie.

Enjoying their easy, breezy romance.

Meanwhile, I don't know what the hell to make of Doug's capriciousness.

He changes his mind on a dime.

Here's the practice. Wait, it's mine. Wait, my daughter is running it. Wait, wait, wait.

Knuckles rap softly on my door. "Hey."

I look up to see Sloane.

"That was quite a surprise," she says as she steps in tentatively then leans against the doorframe.

I heave a sigh. "He seems to love surprising me. First, I think he's going to retire and let me buy him out. But nope, he's bringing you in. Then, I think he's found out about us. But nope, he's jetting off to Europe. And nope, I can't buy the practice, because we're running it together. Because he declared it so," I say, more vitriol in my tone than I intended.

More bitterness than I want her to hear.

Sloane tenses but nods, taking it on the chin. "It's frustrating. I understand."

"I thought things were going to be one way, and now it's another, and he does whatever he wants," I blurt. "I don't know what he expects from me sometimes. The man is always moving goalposts, ever since he started talking retirement. He's a great vet, and he was a great mentor when I needed one, but lately, he's been making me jump through hoops with no warning they're coming my way."

"Would it help if I worked elsewhere? Do you want me to operate Best Friends out of a different space?"

I meet her gaze, give her a *you can't be serious* look. "No. I don't want that."

But as soon as the words come out, I do want that. Because I don't know how the hell to make this work. To balance running the practice, and running it with her, and not falling further and further in love with her every single day.

I glance at the photo of my dad. What would he do?

He'd keep his act together.

I have a clinic to run. Patients to tend to. Clients who need me to be at the top of my game. I can't take care of their four-legged family members if I keep thinking with my dick.

And that's what I've been doing.

I've been playing a no-strings-attached game when I have a real business to manage, one with all sorts of strings, which are wildly entangled.

I drag a hand through my hair. "I don't know how to keep working in the same space with you and not want to bring you into my office every second and kiss the breath out of you," I say, even though that barely covers the truth of my feelings.

The reality is I don't know how to work with her and not tell her that I've fallen so hard and gotten in so deep that I can't tell up from down anymore.

"Do you want to cool things off? That was always the plan," she offers, her tone carefully even, as if she's modulating it.

Do I want to? No fucking way. Do I have to, so I don't crack open my heart every time I see her?

So I can run this business like an adult?

So I can make responsible choices?

I glance at the wall, at the floor, at the door. I dig deep, wishing there were a magic token or key. "I want to do what's right for this clinic. I want to run it like a professional. I can't think straight when my head is full of wanting you, of constantly wanting to get my hands on you. And now he wants us to run it together, so we're going to be working even more closely."

I stand and walk around the desk, wishing I could take her in my arms. Her lips quiver, and she purses them tightly.

"We always planned for this to be a one-week trip. I guess we got to Tahiti and back sooner."

She licks her lips then nods with a jerky motion. "You definitely got me there." She swallows, and it sounds like her throat catches. "I need to go."

She turns and leaves.

Later, when I go home, I tell myself I did the right thing.

I call bullshit on myself.

How can this be right when everything feels wrong?

40

Working with a woman you can't have is awesome.

Said no one ever.

But a man's got to do what a man's got to do.

The next day, I have to go to work.

I treat patients, tightly focused on the needs of my four-legged clientele all morning, saying a curt hello to Sloane when I see her.

Apricat's new owner—since he was adopted quickly from the rescue—comes in that afternoon for a follow-up. The redhead is nervous and kind, asking a ton of questions about her cat. I reassure her that all is well in kitty land. "I promise—the little guy is doing great."

A little later, Quinn and his person arrive. I give that cat a thorough exam and pronounce him on the mend. When I escort the owner out of the exam room, Sloane is in the reception area with Sam, deep in discussion, maybe about a barista, maybe about a band.

I don't know.

I don't try to listen.

But Quinn does. As soon as he hears Sloane's voice, he meows and scrabbles at his crate door. "Meow!"

Sloane spins around, a smile lighting up her face. "Hey, Quinn. I missed you, buddy," she says. "You sure look good."

Kneeling down, she pets him through the front of his carrier. My heart speeds up, running toward her. It handsprings in my chest when she sings, *"After you've gone and left me cryin'. After you've gone, there's no denyin'. You'll feel blue, you'll feel sad."*

She raises her face on the last line, catching my gaze for a fleeting moment.

It's the same for me, I want to say. It's absolutely the same.

Sloane Elizabeth's Post-It Note for Yet Another Day

1. Chin up.

2. Eyes on the prize.

3. Keep going.

4. Be strong. Everything is fine. Everything is fine. Repeat after me—everything is fine.

5. After all, you found a home for Mr. Fox plus five new animals this week alone.

6. Keep thinking about that.

7. Keep saying it.

Damn.

Music is so much better when love has kicked the shit out of you. I'm rocking my set tonight at the Lucky Spot.

This Midtown watering hole is owned by my cousin Nick's good buddy Spencer, and Spencer's wife, Charlotte. They expanded and added a lounge to their bar, and now and then I sing here.

I finish out my set with Harry Connick Jr., then make my way to the table where my crew is waiting. Nick's wife, Harper, touches my arm and makes a sizzling sound. "You are on fire, A Good Man," she says.

I smile faintly. "Thank you very much," I say in my best Elvis impression.

Spencer and Charlotte are at the table too, and so are Jason and Truly, along with Herb and Olivia. The bartender brings us drinks, and we thank her, then I take a swallow of my whiskey.

Spencer claps me on the shoulder. "Such a shame you have no talent."

Charlotte glances at her husband, then at Truly and Harper. "Can you imagine if he could croon for real? A hot singing vet? He'd win hearts everywhere. It's a good thing you can't sing for shit," she says.

"He'd win all the ladies if he could croon halfway decently," Jason remarks.

Truly jumps in. "We'll just leave the lady-winning to you, Jason."

Jason leans across the table, giving my sister a flirty stare. "But you know you're the one I *truly* want."

My sister rolls her eyes. "As if I'd give you the time of day."

Charlotte laughs, pointing from Truly to Jason. "Are you two doing this again? That thing where you flirt but pretend you're not flirting?"

Truly crosses her arms indignantly. "I do not flirt with him."

Jason informs the whole group, "She definitely flirts with me."

Harper pats his arm. "Just ask the woman out. Put us out of our misery."

Jason laughs. "It's much more fun this way."

I sit back and drink my whiskey, observing the theater of my friends, especially since I don't think a damn thing will ever happen with Jason and Truly, despite the rampant flirting. There are plenty of reasons why it won't happen, or, really one reason, but that's a story for another time. For now, I do my best to enjoy their antics while I wish a certain someone could be here.

"So," Olivia says, tapping the table with her nails and staring at me like she just read my mind, "how's everything going with your lovely lady?"

I shake my head adamantly. "It's not going."

Herb frowns like that's confusing. "Hold on. Is this the sweatshirt woman? You guys looked like you were together when we last saw you."

Truly jumps in, squeezing my arm, trying to deflect. "How about them Yankees?"

Subtle. But I choke out a mirthless laugh and answer my buddy. "We had a short fling. Her dad is my business partner. We work together in close quarters. End of story. It's not going to work."

Harper leans across the table and puts a hand on my forehead. "Yes, you do have a temperature."

Charlotte studies me quizzically. "But you love her, so why aren't you going after her?"

I cock my head to give her a sideways stare. "Did I say I loved her?"

She rolls her eyes. "It's obvious."

Olivia nods. "It was certainly obvious when we saw you. You absolutely do need to go after her."

"Didn't you guys hear what I just said? There are a ton of issues in the way. We work together every day. I have employees to supervise. Her dad is my business partner," I emphasize once again. "Hell, the man told me she was off-limits more than once."

Jason leans forward, giving me a hard stare. "Let's be honest—you've never been this sullen before over a woman. You've broken up with others and been more fun than a barrel of monkeys. Maybe it's worth taking a good look at all those *issues*." He sketches air quotes. "Are they truly still relative? Is she really still off-limits, seven years later, after all you've proven to Doug?"

Nick coughs and points his thumb at Harper. "I fell for my best friend's sister. We figured it out."

Spencer drapes his arm around his lovely wife. "We own a bar together. And we were best friends. Yet we still made it work."

Charlotte leans her head against his cheek. "You forgot to mention that you were a total playboy too."

He drops a kiss to her forehead. "I forgot to mention it because I've completely forgotten any part of my life that existed before you."

Herb laughs. "Good answer, man." He turns to me. "Our story is simpler. We dug each other from the start, and we didn't let anything stand in the way."

Olivia points at me. "Maybe that's what you should be doing."

But that's easy for them to say when they're here on the other side of their love stories. Whereas I bet there's a bar somewhere in this city, full of guys and gals who could tell tales just like mine.

The ones that don't have such happy endings.

43

Sloane Elizabeth's Texts

Sloane: I'm miserable.

Piper: I know, hon.

Sloane: What do I do? What would you tell one of your
clients in my situation?

Piper: Well, I'm a wedding planner, not a couples
counselor. And usually my brides have already
resolved their issues.

Sloane: I know that! Back it up to before they resolve
it. Pretend you're giving advice, since I KNOW they
ask you for it. :)

Piper: I would tell them what I'm about to tell you.

Sloane: And that is?

Piper: Go get your happily ever after, bitch!

Sloane: Enough said.

44

A few days later, I finish jujitsu, exhausted, muscles aching, but at the top of my form.

Jason glances at my sister as the three of us leave, heading down the block. "Should we tell him?"

I arch an eyebrow. "Tell me what?"

"We had the tournament this weekend. We talked about you," Truly says.

I stop to face them. "How was the tournament?"

"I won," they both say in unison.

"Congrats."

"But listen, here's the thing," Jason says, patting me on the chest. "We need you to get your shit together."

"Yeah, tell me something I don't know," I say drily.

He shakes his head. "You don't get it. The problem is, you're too good."

Truly chimes in. "You sing better now than you did before things ended with Sloane."

Jason takes his turn. "You play softball better than anyone now."

Truly swings once more. "And you're better at jujitsu than you've ever been. It's just not fair. You were already great at all those things beforehand, and you aren't allowed to be astronomically better now that you've been pummeled by love."

Jason waves in the general direction of the rest of Manhattan. "We need you to become human again. You're making all of us look bad with your excellence, even if it benefits us as your teammates. We don't care. Because it's not benefiting you. Go resolve your stuff with your woman."

I sigh, wishing it were that simple. "How do you want me to do that?"

Truly parks her hands on her hips. "That's up to you, but do it, and do it soon. I need to kick your ass in class again."

But I don't know how the hell I'm supposed to be "ass-kickable" again. I don't have any answers.

I head to the place where I feel most myself, where I know how to solve problems. Maybe that'll give me a flash of clarity. I go to the clinic, making calls to clients, inquiring how their little four-legged family members are doing after surgeries and procedures. I check on paperwork. I answer emails.

But none of that makes me any happier.

None of that soothes the ache in my heart.

I turn and talk to the photo of my dad. "So there's

this girl. I work with her. In the same damn space. I'm madly in love with her. What would you do, Dad?"

I close my eyes, wishing to hear him, longing for his advice. It's been eighteen years, but that hasn't stopped me from wanting it. I try to listen to what he might tell me.

A throat clears. "Tell her father you're in love with her."

In a flash, I sit up straight, open my eyes, and stare at Jonathan, who's standing in the doorway of my office.

"What are you doing here?"

"Sam left her phone, and I came to pick it up for her."

"That was nice of you."

"That's what men and women do for each other when they like each other. They help each other. They tell each other things. They do things for each other. You could do that for Sloane, too, if you would actually take the next step and make things happen."

Up is down. Right is left. Everything is inside out. "Jonathan, are you seriously giving me relationship advice?"

He nods vigorously. "Just tell Doug. Go for it. I swear, your generation makes such a big deal of everything."

I scoff. "You do realize I'm only nine years older than you? That's hardly a generation."

"Feels like a lifetime."

"And you do realize you want me to pay your vet school bills?"

He smiles, a big, cheesy grin. "I do. I do want you to pay my vet school bills. But I also want you to be happy. I saw how you were with Sloane. I don't know what the big deal is. Just go figure it out." He gives a quick wave. "I need to jet. The woman wants me."

He leaves, and I'm all alone.

I stare at the photo once more, but this time I don't need to ask. I know what my dad would tell me. He put my mother first. He put us first. He put love first.

He prioritized that over his practice. Maybe that's why he was never able to open his own clinic.

Because work wasn't his first love.

He was excellent at his job, but he ended each day at five and came home to be with us and my mom. He savored every moment of the years they had together.

Funny—that's what Doug is doing now too. *Savoring.*

I'm the one who's been obsessed with work. Driven mad by a dream my dad never asked me to fulfill.

Maybe he *had* his biggest dreams—his wife and his family—and having his own clinic wasn't worth sacrificing those things.

He wouldn't want me to chase a dream if it made me feel so damn empty.

Right now, that's how I feel without her. Like a part of me is missing. A part she irrevocably owns.

A part I need back desperately, and I need her to bring it back to me, and to say it when she does.

Because she's the dream.

I grab my phone and dial Doug's number, but it goes to voicemail. I bet he's already left for his trip.

I can't do anything to fix this here, so I get the hell out of the office.

45

I go in the direction of my dreams.

I have to earn the right to tell Sloane I love her. To do that, I need to clear a big hurdle. Even though it's late, I call a Lyft and head uptown to Doug's place, stopping in the lobby at the concierge desk, hoping he's not taxiing at the airport, ready for takeoff. The man rings Doug's apartment, and I cross my fingers, sending a tense prayer out to the universe that my business partner is still in town.

I wait.

Then I pump a fist when the concierge says into the phone, "There's a Malone Goodman here to see you, sir."

I wait an interminable amount of time for the concierge to nod and tell me to head to the elevator.

When I press the button, it takes a decade till the elevator arrives. I step inside, just as the other elevator shows up too. The door closes and I will it to shoot up seven stories, lightning fast, to make up the time.

I haven't planned a speech or mapped out a detailed presentation. I march down the hallway and arrive at Doug's door unrehearsed. I take a deep breath, letting it fill me with strength and courage.

I don't know how Sloane is going to react when I finally tell her how I feel. But I know that you can't fix a problem if you don't start at the beginning. There's a process. A way to do things. You don't get to the end of the song if you haven't sung the beginning. You don't finish the surgery if you haven't begun it. You have to do your job in the right order.

Maybe this is the order I should've followed years ago.

But I'm going to follow it now—my relationship with Doug came first, so I have to tell him before I tell her.

I knock on the door. He opens it, shooting me a quizzical look then smiling. "Hey, Malone. Come on in."

I step inside and jump off the cliff. "I'm glad you haven't left yet because I need to tell you I'm madly in love with your daughter. I have been for some time. I'm not asking your permission to pursue a relationship with her, because I'm going to pursue it anyway. I know you once told me not to get any ideas, but I'm crazy in love with her, so that ship has sailed."

Wow. That felt good. That felt freeing, like I'm ten pounds lighter.

Doug's lips twitch. Someone else chuckles. A feminine voice calls out from the living room: "I told you so."

Doug opens the door farther, and Helena strides over and wraps me in a hug. "I've been telling him for the longest time that I thought you and Sloane would make a great couple."

Doug points at her proudly. "She's always right."

Helena drops a kiss on his cheek. "I'm always right."

Doug parks his hands on his hips, staring at me. "What are you going to do about it, Malone? Are you going to go find her and tell her?"

I part my lips but no words come. I'm flabbergasted. I didn't expect this response. Reflexively, I rub my jaw. I expected he'd slam a fist into my face or tell me *not over his dead body*.

I try again to speak, managing only a strangled "But . . ."

Doug laughs. "Cat got your tongue?"

I sputter, "Sir, I just . . . I didn't think."

He claps me on the shoulder. "You thought I didn't know. You thought I'd have a problem with it."

"Well, you did tell me not to get any ideas when you hired me."

"Exactly. But that was seven years ago. Of course I didn't want you going after her then. You were just starting with me."

I wisely keep my mouth shut about when my feelings started, as Doug keeps talking.

"But over the years, I've gotten to know you. I've seen you change. You seemed like something of a Casanova at first, but then I came to know other sides of you. I saw how you cared not just for the animals, but for the employees, for the business. I saw how you look out for your mom. How you spend time with your sister. You care deeply for the people in your life. You're a good man, Malone."

"Thank you sir," I say, still shocked that he's giving me his blessing when I never thought I'd have it offered so willingly.

"Truth be told, once Sloane started working in the practice, I kept thinking you two might be a good fit."

I shake my head in surprise. "You did?"

He nods, pleased with his matchmaker instincts, it seems. "But as for you, you just thought you should stuff your feelings deep down inside and ignore them. Right?"

Nailed it. "I suppose that's what I thought."

Helena laughs. "And how's that working out for you?"

I shake my head. "Not very well."

"I appreciate you telling me," Doug says. "I think it's fantastic. The young vet and the animal rescuer. I can't think of a more perfect combination. You'll be good to my daughter. I'm just glad you had the common sense to figure it out quickly."

I chuckle silently.

"And to tell me," Doug adds.

If he only knew how long it's truly taken.

"Me too," I say. "Thank you, Doug. I can't thank you enough."

He clears his throat. "Listen, I owe you an apology. I know I've been all over the place—retiring, not retiring, cutting back, taking off for my trip tomorrow. It's probably been frustrating from time to time." He tugs Helena in closer. "But that's because I've been trying to decide what to do next—work or spend more time with this lovely woman. It took me a long damn time to find the right one. I have her now, and there's nothing that matters more to me than her happiness. I finally know that's what I should be prioritizing." He stares at me, import in his eyes. "And there's nothing that should matter more to you. I have a feeling that's what your dad would tell you too."

I smile. That rings so true with my instincts about my Dad. I'm confident in that truth when I say, "I'm pretty sure he would."

Helena sets her hands on my shoulders, spins me around, and pushes me out the door. "Go get your girl."

I head toward the door, ready to call Sloane and jet to her place, when I hear Helena on the phone. "Oh good. Glad I caught you. Just tell the cabbie to turn around and then wait in the lobby, hon. He's coming right down."

I swivel around. "She was here?"

Doug smiles. "Yeah. She came by a few minutes ago. Left right before you arrived. But I'm going to let her tell you what she said."

"Good thing she didn't get too far away," Helena adds.

"It sure is."

I run down the hallway, stab the elevator button, and fly downstairs, where I find her in the lobby walking toward me. Perfect timing with the cab.

Her lips are curved in a wild grin. Her flats click against the marble with purpose. Her eyes brim with anticipation and hope.

I don't waste any time.

I march up to her, cup her cheeks, and make a declaration. "Sloane, I am madly in love with you, and I want us to go to Tahiti every single night."

46

"Take me there."

My God, are there any better words?

She kisses me back, tender and loving, making my head spin, my bones hum.

She breaks the kiss, and words spill out like she's desperate to set them free. "I'm so in love with you, Malone. I came here tonight to tell my dad."

My grin can't be contained. "I did the same. I couldn't take it anymore. I need you. I need you every night. I love you so damn much, and I can't let you get away a second time."

She throws her arms around my neck and threads her fingers in my hair, tugging me in for another soft kiss that quickly turns rough.

My tiger.

She is indeed.

"It's the same for me," she says, her voice nearly

breaking. "I wanted to tell you I was in love with you. I wanted to say I didn't want us to end. But then . . ."

"I was an idiot. I thought I couldn't juggle it all. I thought I had to focus only on work."

"I love what I do too . . . but I've been miserable without you. When we were together, it was never just about the sex for me. It was you, it was us—it was everything."

My heart thunders in my chest, beating furiously, just for her. "It was never just sex for me either. Since the night I bumped into you on the street, I think I've been falling in love with you."

"Not to one-up you, but I was falling in love with you seven years ago," she says, her voice as soft as a feather, her gorgeous words rushing through my body.

"Show off," I whisper.

"I'm just saying . . . you're kind of the perfect man for me. I think I was always supposed to be yours."

"You're mine now. All mine. I'm not letting you get away ever again."

She curls her hand tighter around the back of my head. "What are we going to do about your work concerns though? We do spend our days in the same space."

I lean back against her hand. "A lot of people enjoy working together. I've loved every second of working with you. *We fit.* And it makes sense." I laugh at my own pigheadedness. "It makes perfect sense to work together."

She smiles from the inside of her soul. "You know what else makes perfect sense?" She tiptoes her fingers through my hair, dirty question marks in her eyes.

I uncurl her hand from my neck and tip my forehead to the door. "Finishing the rest of our unfinished business."

Twenty minutes later, we're at my place, the door slamming shut as we grab at each other.

Hands, lips, arms.

We tangle together, shedding clothes, keys, her purse in a flurry as we make our way to the bed. I tug her down on top of me, reaching for a condom on the nightstand when she clasps her hand over mine. "I'm on the pill, and I'm clean."

I groan. "Same here."

I claim her mouth, kissing her, consuming her, touching her, stroking her decadent body everywhere till she's so damn wet and ready.

She moves beneath me, opening her legs, and I nearly combust. The sight of her, ready to have me again, is spectacular.

I settle between her thighs, gliding the head of my cock through her slick heat, making her tremble, making her beg.

She arches her back and pleads, "Please. Now. I need you."

If I've learned anything, it's to listen to the woman. I sink inside her.

It's heady and intense, and we fit together so damn

well. Lifting her knees up higher, she opens herself more. I rock into her, swiveling my hips, thrusting deeper. Taking her hands in mine, I slide them above her head.

She arches her back. "Yes, like that. I love it like that."

And we find our rhythm, find our pace. We discover each other as we lose ourselves in the pleasure, in the motion, in the sheer ecstasy of finally coming together like this.

She grabs my ass, pulling me deeper, breathing harder, louder.

I listen to her cues. They tell me to pick up the pace the slightest bit. To fuck her hard. To send her over the edge. That's what she needs.

She cries out.

Yes.

So good.

I'm there.

Oh God, oh God, oh God.

YESSSSSS.

She shudders from head to toe, and I'm consumed to the marrow with desire.

I'm done.

I follow her there, joining her in the blissful oblivion of release.

And savoring the prize too.

The medal, of course.

Not that there was a contest. But I have indeed

successfully taken this woman to the summit of O Town, thank you very much.

Yup, I'm going to enjoy this moment at the top of the podium, and I'm also going to get her here every single time now that I know the path.

Soon she opens her eyes, smiling happily at me. "That reminds me."

I prop my head in my hand. "Of what?"

"I made something for you. A little gift." She hops out of bed, heads to the hall, and returns, clutching her purse and wearing an impish grin.

She dips her hand into her bag and tells me to close my eyes. I do as I'm told.

When she lets me open them, she's standing at the foot of the bed, dangling a pair of purple socks. "For you. Put them on."

Laughing, I sit up. "You want me to put them on now? To wear nothing but socks?"

"It's sexy, you said."

I shake my head. "It's sexy on you. It's not sexy on me."

She turns the socks around, showing me the bottoms.

I crack up and nod. "Those . . . those I'll put on."

A minute later, I lie back in bed with the love of my life and the socks she made me on my feet, the words *Satisfaction Guaranteed* on my soles.

"You *so* look sexy in nothing but socks," she says, snuggling against me.

"Yeah, I probably do."

After all, sexy is about giving satisfaction, and I know that's what I've done for the woman in my arms.

47

**Sloane Elizabeth's Voice Memo to Self on EVERY-
THING YOU NEED TO DO THIS MONTH**

La, la, la, la, la.

Don't forget to finish packing.

In between, you know, whistling a happy tune every freaking second.

Also, lingerie, lingerie, lingerie.

Side note: who knew parading around in sexy lingerie every night for your man could be so fun? Okay, probably a lot of women knew that. BUT! Now you get to do it, and oh hell yeah, it is fun.

So is the prospect of moving in with him.

Wait!

Idea!

There's something we can do when we move in together.

Girl, you are seriously brilliant.

48

"Exactly! That's exactly the approach I would have taken with this respiratory issue." I offer a fist to Jonathan for bumping, and he knocks back. We're in my office, reviewing his initial classwork during the lunch break.

"Thank you. You're not too shabby at this whole vet thing," he deadpans.

"Good to know. Maybe I'll pursue it as a career."

He points at me like I just came up with a brilliant idea. "Consider that. Hell, maybe even run a clinic."

I roll my eyes. "Don't get ahead of yourself there."

But the truth is, I am running this place, and it's great.

Doug's been in Europe for a month now, and he sends us photos via email a couple times a week. Pictures at a cafe in Paris, shots of the two of them on the streets of Barcelona. I have to say, he does look

like the happiest man alive, gallivanting around
Europe with his bride.

But wait. That's not true.

I'm pretty sure that title belongs to me.

Working with Sloane has turned out to be everything we'd hoped for. We click. We help each other.
We give each other space when we need it, and we
offer support when things go wrong.

I suppose the real key to working well together is
knowing we're not going to end. The certainty that
we're together makes us unshakeable.

That has made all the difference.

Plus, she's moving in tonight, and I can't wait to
have her in my apartment all the time. I've been
enjoying the hell out of her nightly lingerie fashion
shows, as well as her healthy appetite for, well, me.

Yeah, life is good when the woman you love wants
to fuck your brains out all the time.

I head to the exam room for the next appointment,
passing Sam and Jonathan at the front desk.

He shows her something on the Yelp app on his
phone. "This place has the best paninis. That's where
we're going tonight, babe."

She shakes her head. "Nope. You need to study. I'll
bring a panini home to you."

"Have I told you that you're the perfect girlfriend?"

"Why, yes, you have, because I am."

I smile to myself. Yup. Some things just work.

* * *

Later that day, Sloane texts, letting me know she's coming in with a cat she sprang from another shelter and asking me to give him an exam and shots.

When she arrives, she looks every bit the rescue queen she is—skinny jeans, boots, and a pullover, her blonde hair piled high in a messy bun. Lugging a cat carrier, she's accompanied by the noisiest feline ever. He sounds like those Meow Mix commercials.

I pat the top of the carrier. "Let's check him out."

We head into the exam room, Jonathan close behind us. Sloane opens the door to the cage, and the melody of meows continues.

As I gingerly slide the cat out, he keeps chatting, almost as if he's singing a tune. "*Meow, meow, meow.*"

He's scruffy, and rough around the edges. But he purrs the second I touch him and doesn't stop the entire exam. He even rubs against me, pushing his chin into my hand, then his whole head.

As I listen to his heart, he stands proudly on all four legs, tail high, cheek sliding against my arm.

"This cat likes you, Dr. Goodman," Jonathan remarks, his tone impressed.

"Don't they all," Sloane says, knowingly. "He's the cat whisperer."

"Dog whisperer too," I add.

Jonathan shakes his head. "But this one? It's a whole new level. It's like he's marking you."

He's not wrong. This cat does indeed seem to like me particularly. He paws at my chest, so I scoop him up, and his purr ignites to a whole new level.

Sloane smiles like she's about the burst.

"What is it?" I ask.

"It's just . . . well, I was leaving a voice memo this morning that I thought it was time for us to get a cat."

My eyes widen. "You were?"

She gestures to the striped tabby in my arms. "But I think the cat has gotten you."

I look down at the feline in my arms. He lets forth another litany of meows, and it appears that I've just been adopted.

* * *

That evening, I'm lying in bed with the Chairman of the Board stretched out next to me, purring. Showing off like only a cat can do. He's the loudest beast I've ever heard, and when he meows, it's a serenade.

I pet his back, and he luxuriates in the moment. He's so shameless. Such a love whore.

But then, I suppose I am too.

Because when Sloane struts into the bedroom showing off her new lingerie—a lacy sky-blue bra and panty set—I scoop up the cat, set him on the floor, and bring my woman next to me.

The Chairman meows his disdain, but he wanders off.

Good thing, because I need this whole bed for what I plan to do to Sloane tonight.

Make her purr so goddamn loud that the cat is impressed.

And that's exactly what I do.

* * *

The next morning, I'm woken by a demanding meow.

I sit up, scrub a hand across my chin, and get out of bed.

In the kitchen, I scoop out some vittles for the Chairman, and he sings his praises as he chows down.

I return to bed, wake Sloane in her favorite way—she does enjoy the morning Os—then take her to breakfast, where we meet my friends at the diner.

Sloane is wearing my sweatshirt again this morning, but she proudly proclaims to Olivia and Herb, "I'm no longer doing the walk of shame."

"And she never will again." I slide in next to her at the booth to enjoy breakfast and everything else about the way our life together is unfolding.

49

A few months later

The lights are low.

The drinks are plentiful.

The crowd is my favorite.

Because it includes her. Sloane's here in the front row like she is at many of my shows.

Tonight though? All the songs are for her.

I'm sure it's patently obvious to the whole crowd that I'm singing to one person.

Especially when my gaze locks with hers on the first line of a Bing Crosby tune.

"Let me call you sweetheart."

Every table is packed, and it's standing room only —word of mouth has been good to us here at Gin Joint —but my set is for Sloane. This song is for Sloane.

"I'm in love with you."

She mouths the words back to me, and that emboldens me.

"Let me hear you whisper that you love me too."

So much, she mouths.

When I finish that serenade, I glide right into the song that made her melt the first night she was here, telling her she looks wonderful tonight. Hell, she looks wonderful *every* night.

I'm pretty sure I'm ready for my final number. I finish with her favorite, "I Don't Stand a Ghost of a Chance with You."

When the music ends, I don't stop. I downshift from singing to talking. "That song is ironic, in a way," I say, my eyes on hers.

She watches me expectantly as I make my way to her, and she whispers back, "It is ironic."

"At first, I didn't think we stood a chance."

"Me either," she says softly.

"But I wanted one."

"So did I."

"And tonight, I want more. I want the opposite of that song."

She gasps quietly then presses her lips together.

I weave past a table, stopping beside the beautiful blonde I love madly. "I want all the chances with you. Now, tomorrow, and forever."

"Oh God," she whispers. "Me too."

I drop down to one knee and take her hand in

mine. "I want to love you for the rest of our lives. Will you marry me, Sloane?"

A tear streaks down one cheek, and she grabs my mic, sets it on the table, and kisses the hell out of me.

I'll take that as a yes.

But even so, when she breaks the kiss, she picks up the mic and confirms to the whole crowd, "Yes. You can have all the second chances you want with me. Tonight, tomorrow, and always."

I slide a ring on her finger as the audience cheers.

I bring her to her feet, dip her, and kiss her once more.

50

Jason

A few months later

Malone takes off early after the softball game tonight.

Which is perfect since I need to chat with Nick without my best mate around.

We head out of the park on the late summer evening, and I clear my throat, then dive headfirst into my request.

"Can we grab a pint? Because I need to pick your brain."

He reaches for his skull, as if protecting his hair. "No! Not the brain. I need that. It's one of my favorite organs."

Laughing, I shake my head. "Listen, it's about your cousin."

Nick furrows his brow. "Malone? Are you having a bro fight with him?"

"The *other* cousin."

"Truly?"

"Yes. Precisely."

"What do you want to know about Truly? Seems you know her pretty well."

"And yet she remains impervious to my charms."

Nick laughs, stroking his beard. "Ah, the plot thickens. You need a little advice in the how-to-win a lady department."

"Correction: I need a little advice in how to win my best mate's sister."

He cocks a brow. "The same best mate's sister who's impervious to your charms."

I nod. "Have I mentioned I love a challenge?"

"That's one helluva hill to climb. We might need two pints."

We head to a pub, order, and roll up our sleeves.

Truly is indeed some kind of challenge. But I'm a determined man, no matter how many hurdles I might face.

EPILOGUE

Sloane

A few more months later

My phone rings.

I'm expecting Piper, since she's helping me with all things wedding-related.

But her name's not the one on the screen as I grab it from the kitchen counter. "Hey, Dad," I say, after I swipe the screen.

Malone looks up from his tablet. It's nine thirty on a Saturday, so I suspect he's reading the news as he usually does on weekend mornings. It's his habit, and I love knowing his habits.

I love knowing him.

Like the fact that his friends rely on him. He sees

them often, whether for softball or jujitsu or basketball.

And that his sister is a hoot, all sassy and fiery and full of love.

That he adores this city, and he'll try anything with me—whether it's a movie, an art gallery, or even dancing. We've been taking swing lessons so we can cut a rug at our wedding.

I love, too, that there's so much more for us yet to discover about each other, and we will.

"How's everything in Italy?" I ask my father as I park myself on a stool at the counter next to my fiancé. I wasn't expecting to hear from my dad for another few days.

Malone grabs me and pulls me onto his lap, whispering. "I want to take you to Tahiti."

I swat him, shushing him. He loves to rile me up when I talk to my father. I swear this man is trouble.

"Tuscany is great," my dad answers. "So great, in fact, that it's giving Helena and me all sorts of ideas."

Malone arches a brow, since he can hear my dad's side of the call.

"What do you mean, Dad?" I feign not knowing, but I suspect where he's heading.

"Why don't you put me on speakerphone? I can tell my son-in-law is there," he says.

Smiling, I turn on the speaker and set the phone on the counter.

"You do know I'm not your son-in-law for another three weeks," Malone remarks.

"I do. I can count. But I already think of you that way."

"And I'm glad you're going to be my father-in-law," he says, and I snuggle up against my man, loving the way his relationship with my dad has evolved.

Once upon a time, my father was his mentor. Then his business partner. Then his roadblock.

Now?

He's just my dad.

Just the father of the woman Malone loves.

It's so much better like this.

Of course, there is still that little matter of the vet clinic. But I smile, since I know something Malone doesn't.

My dad clears his throat. "I was thinking of a wedding present for you two."

Malone answers. "You don't have to get us anything, Doug. After all, I kind of have the last laugh. I'm marrying your daughter." A little twinkle crosses his eyes.

I rein in a smirk.

My dad chuckles. "I suppose that's true. But I have something for the two of you, and I'm giving it to you now."

Malone shoots me a curious look. I simply shrug, like I don't know what it is.

"I'm giving you both the practice. It's yours. Enjoy."

Malone's jaw drops, and he coughs in surprise. "Excuse me?"

"It's yours. I'm not selling you my half. I'm giving it to the two of you. Be good to my daughter for the rest of your life."

"Of course. I will. I absolutely will. This is incredible. Thank you."

My dad says goodbye and hangs up.

Malone tugs me in closer and runs his fingers across my cheek. "I can't believe that. I really can't. Did you know about this?"

"He mentioned it to me last night. Do you like it?"

Malone shakes his head, a smile lighting up his whole face. No, the whole city. "I love it. It's incredible." He presses a kiss to my forehead then pulls back, wonder in his eyes. "I can't believe we're going to keep running it together. The clinic and the rescue. This is a dream come true."

"It's ours. It's sort of perfect, isn't it?"

"It's completely perfect. Like it was meant to be."

"That's how I feel about you."

He cups my cheeks and kisses me again, then laughs. "I guess we really are stuck together."

I laugh and swat his elbow. "Yes, we are."

"And that's exactly where I want to be."

This, here with him? That's the dream.

ANOTHER EPILOGUE

Malone

Some men believe the ability to make a woman purr is the apex of male performance.

That if you achieve such a victory in bed, you're the king of studs, the master of men.

I call bullshit.

Look, I *can* make my woman purr. Hell, I do it every single night.

But that's only one of the many things I do for her.

I satisfy her in other ways. In all the ways. By treating her right. By listening to her. By creating this fantastic life together where we work hard and we play hard.

Where we encourage each other in all our dreams.

Where we create new dreams together.

She makes me want to sing all the love songs in the world to her.

She deserves them.

As for me? Well, the socks really do say it all.

Fortunately, she's made me several pairs, so I can wear her favorite saying each day of the week and then deliver it to her every night.

But I'm not just a satisfaction guaranteed kind of guy in the bedroom. That's a promise to her in every way.

It's one I plan to deliver on each day.

Right now though? I have a plane to catch. We're going to Tahiti for our honeymoon.

AND ANOTHER EPILOGUE

Sloane

A few months later

I pour a glass of champagne and bring it to the couch, tucking my feet under me.

Malone settles in at the baby grand, exactly where I want him.

"Champagne, you, a little music," I say, a smile on my lips as I take a drink.

"What could be better?" he muses as he locks his gaze with mine. "Wait, should I join you on the couch?"

I huff. "Stop teasing me."

"But I thought you liked me next to you."

I narrow my eyes and point to the piano. "I want my special preview."

"Are you sure?"

I laugh. "You're such a tease. Just play."

"Just one song?"

I shake my head. "You're giving me a preview of the whole album, mister."

In a few days, Malone is headed into a studio to record an album of old standards. I might have been instrumental in encouraging him to do it. Sometimes he needs a little push from me, and I'm all too happy to give it to him. This is one part of him I don't mind sharing.

"If you insist," he says, then taps out a few notes.

"'The Curse of an Aching Heart.' Play it for me."

"As you wish."

He sings it for me, and the song weaves its way through my body.

I clap when he finishes, leap up from the couch, and give him a kiss. "It's so sad, it kills me."

"Some of the best songs are the sad ones."

"It's so true. That's why we connect with them so much—somehow the music makes an aching heart better."

"Your heart better not be aching."

I run a hand through his hair. "Mine is full. It'll be even fuller if you play me the next one."

"Anything for you."

I return to the couch, savor another sip of champagne, and then give him my full attention as he plays "After You've Gone" just for me.

When he's done, I wipe a rebel tear from my cheek.

"Did it make you cry?"

"A little."

He shoots me a devilish smile.

"That makes you happy, you cruel man?"

"It means I'm doing my job."

"You are definitely doing your job. You're making me cry and making me swoon at the same damn time."

"Let's see if I can do it once more, then."

"I have no doubt. What's the next one for your album?"

"Just a little song that I'm pretty sure made you fall for me once upon a time."

"Is that so?"

"If memory serves, you heard me sing it to a cat."

"Ah! Yes, I do recall you charming that pussycat with 'Baby Won't You Please Come Home.'"

"I'm pretty sure it worked on you too."

"Is that so?"

"Let's give it a shot and find out."

And he's right. His latest rendition does the trick.

I'm leaning on the piano, moony-eyed, heart pitter-pattering, ready for him. "It worked."

"Don't you want to hear the rest of the songs for my album?"

"Later. I have other plans for you now."

"Far be it from me to withhold your satisfaction."

THE END

Eager for Jason and Truly's romance? Want to know how the sexy Brit plans to win his best friend's sister's heart? (Guess what? He'll have a lot of hurdles to cross, but get ready for fake dates and secrets!) You won't want to miss INSTANT GRATIFICATION!

Sign up for my newsletter to receive an alert when these sexy new books are available!

. . .

A portion of the proceeds from all sales of Satisfaction Guaranteed will be donated to animal rescue organizations. Thank you for purchasing this book!

ACKNOWLEDGEMENTS

All songs with lyrics cited in this novel are in the public domain.

- —"The Curse of an Aching Heart," music by Al Piantadosi, words by Henry Fink, from 1913
- — "After You've Gone," words by Henry Creamer, music by Turner Layton, from 1918
- —"Baby, Won't You Please Come Home," words and music by Clarence Williams and Charles Warfield, from 1919
- —"I Ain't Got Nobody (And Nobody Cares for Me), music by Spencer Williams and Dave Peyton, words by Roger Graham, from 1915
- — "After You Get What You Want, You

Don't Want It," words and music by Irving
Berlin, from 1920
- —"Let Me Call You Sweetheart," music by
Leo Friedman, words by Beth Slater
Whitson, from 1910
- —"I'm Always Chasing Rainbows," music
by Harry Carroll, words by Joe McCarthy,
from 1918

Abiding thanks to Public Domain Information Project
at PDinfo.com for insight on public domain music,
and to researcher Tiffany Tyer, for tracking down
these tunes.

As always, thank you to Helen for the beautiful cover,
and the amazing feedback. And to Kim, Lauren, Lynn,
Virginia, Jen, Karen, RC, Janice and Steph. Thank you
to Cheryl for the vet feedback.

And thank you to my readers for loving books and
to my pets for providing inspiration.

ALSO BY LAUREN BLAKELY

FULL PACKAGE, the #1 New York Times Bestselling
romantic comedy!

BIG ROCK, the hit New York Times Bestselling standalone
romantic comedy!

MISTER O, also a New York Times Bestselling standalone
romantic comedy!

WELL HUNG, a New York Times Bestselling standalone
romantic comedy!

JOY RIDE, a USA Today Bestselling standalone romantic
comedy!

HARD WOOD, a USA Today Bestselling standalone
romantic comedy!

THE SEXY ONE, a New York Times Bestselling bestselling
standalone romance!

THE HOT ONE, a USA Today Bestselling bestselling
standalone romance!

THE KNOCKED UP PLAN, a multi-week USA Today and
Amazon Charts Bestselling bestselling standalone romance!

MOST VALUABLE PLAYBOY, a sexy multi-week USA

Today Bestselling sports romance! And its companion sports romance, MOST LIKELY TO SCORE!

THE V CARD, a USA Today Bestselling sinfully sexy romantic comedy!

WANDERLUST, a USA Today Bestselling contemporary romance!

COME AS YOU ARE, a Wall Street Journal and multi-week USA Today Bestselling contemporary romance!

PART-TIME LOVER, a multi-week USA Today Bestselling contemporary romance!

UNBREAK MY HEART, an emotional second chance USA Today Bestselling contemporary romance!

BEST LAID PLANS, a sexy friends-to-lovers USA Today Bestselling romance!

The Heartbreakers! The USA Today and WSJ Bestselling rock star series of standalone!

The New York Times and USA Today Bestselling Seductive Nights series including *Night After Night, After This Night,* and *One More Night*

And the two standalone romance novels in the Joy Delivered Duet, *Nights With Him* and Forbidden Nights, both New York Times and USA Today Bestsellers!

Sweet Sinful Nights, Sinful Desire, Sinful Longing and Sinful Love, the complete New York Times Bestselling high-heat romantic suspense series that spins off from Seductive Nights!

Playing With Her Heart, a

USA Today bestseller, and a sexy Seductive Nights spin-off standalone! (Davis and Jill's romance)

21 Stolen Kisses, the USA Today Bestselling forbidden new adult romance!

Caught Up In Us, a New York Times and

USA Today Bestseller! (Kat and Bryan's romance!)

Pretending He's Mine, a Barnes & Noble and

iBooks Bestseller! (Reeve & Sutton's romance)

My USA Today bestselling

No Regrets series that includes

The Thrill of It

(Meet Harley and Trey)

and its sequel

Every Second With You

My New York Times and USA Today

Bestselling Fighting Fire series that includes

Burn For Me

(Smith and Jamie's romance!)

Melt for Him

(Megan and Becker's romance!)

and *Consumed by You*

(Travis and Cara's romance!)

The Sapphire Affair series...

The Sapphire Affair

The Sapphire Heist

Out of Bounds

A New York Times Bestselling sexy sports romance

The Only One

A second chance love story!

Stud Finder

A sexy, flirty romance!

CONTACT

I love hearing from readers! You can find me on Twitter at LaurenBlakely3, Instagram at LaurenBlakelyBooks, Facebook at LaurenBlakelyBooks, or online at LaurenBlakely.com. You can also email me at laurenblakelybooks@gmail.com

Made in the USA
San Bernardino, CA
10 July 2019